OUT OF THE BLUE

Also by James McManus

Antonio Salazar Is Dead
Curtains
Chin Music
Ghost Waves

OUT OF THE BLUE

James McManus

GROVE PRESS
New York

Copyright © 1984 by James McManus

First published by Crown Publishers, 1984

All rights reserved.

No part of this book may be reproduced, stored in a retrieval system, or transmitted in any form, by any means, including mechanical, electronic, photocopying, recording or otherwise, without prior written permission of the publisher.

The name Grove Press and the colophon printed on the title page and outside of this book are trademarks registered in the U.S. Patent and Trademark Office and in other countries.

Published by Grove Press
a division of Wheatland Corporation
841 Broadway
New York, N.Y. 10003

Library of Congress Cataloging-in-Publication Data

McManus, James.
    Out of the blue/by James McManus. —1st Evergreen ed.
      p. cm.
    ISBN 0-8021-3154-9 (alk. paper)
    I. Title.
[PS3563.C38608   1989]   88-31830
813'.54—dc19   CIP

Designed by Irving Perkins Associates

Manufactured in the United States of America

This book is printed on acid-free paper.

First Evergreen Edition 1989

10 9 8 7 6 5 4 3 2 1

I know when one is dead,
and when one lives.
LEAR

OUT OF THE BLUE

H UBBARD WOODS, ILLINOIS, viewed, moving north, from the height of the flight of a helicopter through the darkness and quiet of 10:39 Sunday evening. There are lights on in most of the houses, a few cars still out on the streets, a couple of half-open gas stations, an uncountable number of trees. To the east, a thin slice of moon reflects off Lake Michigan.

THE LIVING ROOM of a small two-bedroom apartment upstairs from V. J. Killian's Hubbard Woods Heating and Plumbing. Jack and Shelley Exley are watching the news and Elizabeth, their five-year-old daughter, is eating a butter cookie, nibbling off alternate nubs until only four of the original eight nubs are left.

Exley gets up, yawns, changes channels, sits back down on the couch. Elizabeth hums. Shelley removes the green rubber bands from the ends of Elizabeth's braids, undoes the strands with her fingers, starts brushing the hair from the bottom.

"Hey, Mom?" says Elizabeth. She bites off a nub. "Is each of the twists in my braids its own separate braid or's it all just one braid?"

"Yeah," says Exley, to Shelley. "I was just wondering the same thing myself."

"I think it's all just one braid," Shelley says. "Just hold still now, okay? Each separate twist is all part of one single braid."

Elizabeth bites off the two final nubs on the cookie. "See?" she says, chewing. She looks up at Exley. "That means I only have two."

"You brush yet?" he says.

"Nope."

"How's the tooth?"

Licking and nibbling, Elizabeth rounds off the edge of what's left of the cookie, careful to keep intact the ring she's just fashioned, then looks through the hole at her father.

"Still loose?" he says.

"Yup."

"Honey, please," Shelley says. "Almost done."

Elizabeth swallows the cookie ring whole with one bite. "Ummm," she says, rubbing her stomach. "Yum."

Exley looks up at the clock. "I think . . ."

Shelley puts down the brush and sits back.

"Still loose," says Elizabeth, turning and facing her mother. "It's *still* kinda loose, Mommy." She pushes one of her lower incisors back and forth with her thumb. " 'ook."

"Hmm."

Elizabeth turns back to her father, grinning, moving her tooth with her tongue now.

"I would say," Exley says, "that it's just about—"

Elizabeth jumps up off the couch. "Good night now Charles Osgood for CBS News." She switches off the TV. "Didn't *you* know it's way past my bedtime *either*?"

"*Way* past," says Shelley.

Exley stands up.

"Can we still read a story tonight?" says Elizabeth.

Exley hoists her up by her armpits. He lets her hang from his neck for a second, makes a big scary face, then crosses his forearms under her rump to support her.

"Just one short short story, Dad? Please?"

"No stories tonight I don't think," Exley says. He lets go with one hand and brushes some crumbs from her robe. "It's much much too late."

"But just one, though, Daddy? Come on." She wedges her forehead between his neck and his shoulder. "Okay?"

"E-beth," says Shelley. She's standing beside them now. "It's already an hour and a half—"

"No stories, E.," Exley says. "Not tonight."

"Then just one real real short tuck-in chat, then?"

Exley carries her down the short hall to the bathroom. "We'll see," he says. "But this is too damn late for you. Really."

She squeezes him. "Yes?"

"Maybe."

"Maybe yes?"

"Maybe," he says. He lets her slide down till her toes touch the small oval rug in front of the sink, lets her go. "Better brush now."

"Yes, a story?"

"Yes, one very short chat. An extremely—"

"Just but *how* short of one?"

"Just brush now," says Exley. "Just brush."

A MUSTANG AND A QUANTUM pull into the dark empty parking lot alongside Hubbard Woods High School.

The Mustang gets parked between two yellow lines, its lights are shut off, its driver climbs out and locks it.

The driver of the Mustang gets into the Quantum and the Quantum pulls out of the parking lot.

Exley pulls back Elizabeth's quilt and lowers her onto her bed. "But it's gotta be a short one," he says.

"Or how about one gonzo one about the book about the golden retrievers?"

He pulls the quilt up to her shoulders and lies down beside her. "Short one, E. We both have to get up now, you know, get up for school in the morning."

"Yeah!" says Elizabeth, jerking her head off the pillow and grinning. "We *both* go to school now."

"All three of us, right? Your mom goes now too."

"*I* know that, Daddy. But what could the chat be tonight?"

"How about . . . what about, about what we could name—"

"What about those two golden puppies from yesterday, my new baby brother or sister and what its name's gonna be maybe, and how many quarters you're gonna put under my pillow when I'm asleep when my tooth loosens out?"

"This pillow right here?"

"I guess," says Elizabeth. Then: "A course this pillow right here!"

Shelley comes in now and switches the lamp off—a small blue night-light stays on—then leans down and kisses Elizabeth. "I think that's the tooth fairy that does that, you know."

"I know," says Elizabeth. "I was just *say*ing it's you guys."

"She was just *say*ing it, Shelley."

"Night now, E.," Shelley says. She rearranges the covers around her. "Us guys'll see you early and fresh."

"Early and fresh, Mom ... Daddy's still gonna chat though, right? Like he promised."

"But just a short one, though, E. We've all got big days in the morning."

Shelley goes out.

"That's what you *al*ways say, Daddy."

"I do?"

"Yeah, man, you do." She touches his nose with her finger. "That's what you say to me each single night."

"Must be true, then."

"Really?"

"Really."

"So but—"

"But really, how much do you think the tooth fairy's gonna leave you?"

"How much? I don't know yet how much."

"Me neither."

"But can the tooth fairy leave you fifty-six dollars?"

"Maybe."

"But how much is that?"

"I don't know about fifty-six dollars, though. For a first tooth that's kind of a lot."

"So but, is fifty-six take away zero ... is how much is that?"

"Fifty-six take away zero?"

Elizabeth nods.

"Think about that. Fifty-six . . . you have fifty-six and you take away none."

"Um . . ."

Exley waits.

"Um . . . come on, Daddy. Tell me."

"Fifty-six take away none . . . is . . ."

"Is . . ."

"Fifty-six."

"It *is*?" says Elizabeth, squinting. "But do you guys have that much in the bank though?"

"I doubt it. But maybe the tooth fairy does."

"She *does*?"

"I think that it might be a secret, though, about exactly how much money she has. Do you know what I mean?"

"I guess so."

"Maybe she only has enough to give you a quarter, though. I don't know."

"But does it depend on how many other kids' teeth loosens out on that night?"

"I guess so," says Exley. He smiles. "I guess it probably *does* work out something like that."

"Or maybe fifty-six quarters, or something like that."

Exley yawns now, turning away from Elizabeth and covering his mouth with his fist.

"When will we know, though?"

"When? You'll know on the same morning after you put your tooth under the pillow. You just reach right back down under here and find out."

"Soon's I wake up it'll be there, you mean?"

"I think so. At least that's how it worked when my first tooth came out."

"How much did *you* get then though, Dad?"

"I think all I got was a nickel."

"Isn't there any way we can find out sooner, though?"

"No way, E. You always have to wait to find out things like this. It's better that way, though, having it be a surprise. It's one of the rules."

"But I *hate* surprises like that, Daddy, ones you always have to wait so long to find out for." She smiles over at him, both eyes wide open, trying to hold back the smile. "I know I'm smiling now, but I'm serious."

"It's serious business," says Exley.

"I'm *very* serious, Daddy," she says. "I really am very serious."

The thin slice of moon reflects off Lake Michigan.

A small blond child stares out the window of a white stucco house.

A man walks a dog along Sheridan Road.

A nurse shimmies out of her Porsche, checks through her purse for her keys, runs up the steps to her porch.

A series of very small waves hit the beach, spread out over the pebbles and sand, then slide back down into the lake.

E<small>XLEY</small> <small>BRUSHES</small> along Shelley's spine with his knuckles as she slips off her plaid woolen skirt. The next day's weather comes over the radio: sunny and breezy, high in the low- to mid-fifties.

Shelley reaches behind her and unhooks her bra, slides it down off her arms. She is twenty weeks pregnant.

From the side, Exley watches.

They rest their hands on each other's shoulders and, their lips barely touching, start kissing.

Shelley turns back then, drapes the bra over the back of a rocker, slips off her white cotton panties. "She asleep yet?"

Reaching around her, Exley turns her left nipple between his thumb and his forefinger, breathes on the back of her neck.

Shelley exhales through her mouth.

All of a sudden Exley says, "*Shit*."

"What?"

"I haven't got any shirts for this week."

Shelley does not turn around. "I thought . . . So what time does Zengeler's open?"

Exley takes off his shirt, grabs a hanger from out of the

closet, hangs the shirt up. "I haven't even taken them in yet."

"Mmm."

Exley gets out of his pants.

"Well . . ."

Exley leans over and brushes her hip with his lips.

"You're right, then," she says, reaching back, stroking him with the side of her wrist.

"What?"

Shelley puts both hands onto her belly, massages herself for a second, slides her hands onto her hips. "You ain't got no shirts for this week."

Exley bites her softly on the back of her thigh, bites her harder. Laurie Anderson's "Walking and Falling" comes on the radio now.

Shelley rotates her palm on his ear. "Trouble city," she says, breathing in. "Funky shirts. She asleep yet?"

He continues to kiss her.

"Is she?"

They do not speak now for more than a minute.

Their breathing gets jagged.

They listen.

Shelley puts her hands on his head and leans back as Exley kneels down in front of her. She breathes out and shivers.

A small fist knocks on the door now.

They look at each other.

"But so, there you are."
"About exactly how long?"
"Too chancy. No way."

MONDAY, THE FIRST DAY of the fourth week of school.

There are seven classrooms, four on one side of the hallway and three on the other, on the first floor of the Hubbard Woods Elementary School. They are arranged in descending order from fourth grade through kindergarten.

The hallway is empty. Various noises and voices can be heard from inside the classrooms. The gray tile floor of the hallway has been waxed just that weekend.

From the first-grade room, the last room on the right, comes the sound of one flute's arpeggios.

Across the hall, on the wall to the left of the door, is a brown leafless tree that's been cut from a large piece of cardboard; there are creases from when it had still been a box. In an arc above its branches, also in cardboard, are the words FALL INTO KINDERGARTEN. Around the base of the tree is a cluster of seventeen maple leaves that have been cut from either scarlet, orange, purple, or yellow construction paper. Each leaf bears the name of one of the kindergartners: Colin, Machiko, John, Lowell, Elizabeth, Kelly, Gordie, Heide, Carlos, Genevieve R., Mark, Audrey, Jimmy, Genevieve W., and Max. The two other names are the names of the teachers: Mrs. Witt and Mrs. Zigulski.

Tentatively, but soon with more confidence, a second flute joins the first one.

Beyond the kindergarten, at the end of the hallway, are three steel-and-glass exit doors, which lead out onto the playground.

The music of two flutes continues.

IT IS COOL OUT, and still, for early October.
Three Hubbard Woods High School cheerleaders, wearing their green-and-white uniforms, are crammed together in the front seat of a small red Datsun station wagon; all three are laughing hysterically. The girl who is driving is smoking a cigarette.
"Old Dan Rather's not half bad himself," says the girl on the right.
They begin to calm down.
"*Oh* yeah," says the driver.
"I Don't Remember" comes on the radio now, and the middle girl turns up the volume. All three girls begin to yodel and shout along with Peter Gabriel, shifting their weight on the seat with the chords, bumping and grinding.
The sun breaks in long streaks and shafts through the trees along Sheridan Road. Its reflection slides jaggedly over the glass of the Datsun and dazzles the left sideview mirror. The leaves on the trees overhead are the colors of the paper leaves outside the kindergarten, only much more spectacular and vivid. To the left, beyond a succession of small hills and mansions and trees, is Lake Michigan.

The girls sing the gibberish chorus along with the backup singers.

Near the Elder Lane Beach they pass a Hubbard Woods squad car with its radar gun pointing north, and they wave. The Datsun is doing three miles over the speed limit.

The girl on the right rolls down her window, lights a cigarette, rests her elbow outside. "It's great out," she says.

The driver just nods.

"Really," says the girl in the middle.

They turn right at Winnetka Avenue and drive past two more blocks of houses; the houses here are not quite so large. The driver rolls down her window five or six inches and tosses her cigarette out.

Two of the gym classes are meeting outside on the tennis courts; there are orange and yellow balls everywhere. The girls honk and wave.

They drive past the high school's main building now, eyes peeled for a parking spot, then turn right at Birch Street. "Once in a Lifetime" comes on now, and the girl on the right whistles and rolls up her window.

They park in the far corner of the big student lot off of Birch; it's the only spot left. They get out, lock both front doors, and begin walking between the two rows of cars toward the school.

Suddenly the girl who'd been driving stops, turns around and says "Jeez," then starts running back toward the Datsun.

The other two call back to her, slapping their thighs, complaining they're "gonna be late."

The driver unlocks the door, rolls the window all the way up, presses the lock button down, and slams the door shut. Then she runs to catch up with her friends.

The girl who'd sat on the right makes a joke now, and all three girls start to laugh.

"This is *no* wave," she says.

As they approach the end of the parking lot, a red-haired boy calls out to them from a third-floor classroom window. His exact words are not comprehensible; it is something about "days in a row."

The girl who'd sat in the middle grimaces, looks at her friends, then calls up to the boy in the window.

Right away the other two girls start to hoot, mimicking the way she'd responded. "*Wha?*" says the driver, raising her voice to a whine and making herself sound gullible and dumb. "*Huh?*"

As the second word leaves her lips there's a loud blast behind them. A light blue Mustang is parked about twenty-five feet from where they are standing; they'd just walked right past it. Its hood is blown off and the entire front end of the car has burst into flames.

All three girls duck down and turn simultaneously. They watch as the Mustang's hood lands on the roof of a car in the opposite row and bounces back up in the air.

"Holy shit."

The driver and the girl who'd sat in the middle begin crawling toward the end of the row. The other girl starts to sob. She is still holding onto her cigarette, pinching it between those two fingers.

There's a second blast now, even louder, as the Mustang's gas tank explodes.

The red-haired boy's face disappears from the window then reappears almost immediately. It's been joined now by two other faces. By this point all three cheerleaders are crouched behind the last car in the row.

An arc of translucent heat shimmers up over what's left of the Mustang. The twisted hood lies on the sidewalk.

A white Quantum drives by on Birch, stops at the corner, turns right.

Dozens of faces appear at the windows along all three floors of the high school.

Thick black smoke rises up over the parking lot.

There is almost no wind, almost silence.

Audrey stands in the center of the carpeted play area, opening and closing her eyes. "I'm hungry," she says.

"Let's draw," says Genevieve Webster. "Let's go draw."

"Hey yeah," Audrey says.

They are surrounded by six large bay windows. Numbers, letters of the alphabet, children's faces in watercolor, and pictures of animals are stapled and taped over the windows and onto the wall space between and beneath them. The bright sun outside lights the room.

Russell is talking to Colin and Mrs. Zigulski and John at one of the tables. It is drawing time. The six low wooden tables are arranged in a rectangle that extends from the play area into the rest of the room.

"Lisa's big now," says Colin. "But not that big because she still has to wear diapers."

"Does your mom let you help change her?" says Mrs. Zigulski.

"Sure does," says Russell. "All the time."

"But doesn't it stink?" says Colin.

"Yup," says Russell. "Sure does."

Kelly, Machiko, Genevieve Rawls, and Elizabeth are using their table to draw. They are silent. Genevieve and

Machiko are drawing their dads; Machiko is making her dad's hair light blue. Kelly and Elizabeth are working on pigs.

"I keep have to unrasing it," says Kelly, rubbing out part of a hand.

"Me too," says Elizabeth. "It's *e*rase it. *E*."

Kelly just looks at her.

"My name isn't Unlizabeth, you know."

Kelly giggles.

Mrs. Witt, Heide, and Max are feeding Mrs. Esther G. Hubbard, the garter snake.

Mrs. Zigulski stands behind Colin. "That's a real good wheel, Colin," she says. "Is that your new bike?"

"Yup," says Colin. "It's a dirt bike."

"I got one too," says Russell. "Mine is gonzo."

Mrs. Zigulski looks up at the clock now. "Do you think you're ready to pass out your snack now, Russell?"

Russell jumps up. "Sure am."

Mrs. Zigulski and Russell go over by the sink and refrigerator. The snack he has brought is a one-gallon jug of apple cider and two large loaves of zucchini bread.

Mrs. Witt comes over to help. Mrs. Zigulski fills paper cups up with the cider while Mrs. Witt slices the bread. Russell takes each slice and places it onto a red-and-white checkered napkin, then arranges the napkins in two neat rows along the edge of one of the tables.

"Did you help your mom bake this?" says Mrs. Witt.

"Sure did," Russell says. He looks at Mrs. Zigulski.

"That must have been fun."

Russell just nods.

"Come and get it now, friends," says Mrs. Witt.

Four of the children are already there at the snack table. Most of the others now stop what they're doing and start heading in that direction.

"I want a whole of one," says Genevieve Webster.

"Me too," says Audrey.

"Look at this delicious zucchini bread that Russell's mom baked for us," says Mrs. Witt.

The children crowd around the small snack table.

"*And* Russell," says Mrs. Zigulski.

Russell starts biting his fingernails. He is smiling.

"Try not to spill your cider now, Mark," says Mrs. Zigulski.

"You too, Heide," says Mrs. Witt.

R̲OOM 216, STEVENSON HALL, the University of Illinois at Chicago. Jack Exley's ten-o'clock section of Comp 101.

"Before I forget," Exley says, standing up. "Pass those comparison and contrast papers in to your left."

There are groans.

"Before he forgets," someone says.

Exley moves to his right and begins gathering together the small piles of essays at the end of each row.

"That thing's due *today*?"

There is laughter.

"Yours is due next Monday, Terry," says Exley. "It's only everyone else's I'm gonna collect now."

"Am I gonna lose points?"

"Kind of looks that way, Terry."

There is laughter.

"About how many?"

"Oh . . . how's about, say, twenty-five percent of the total."

"But I was sick, I think, on the day you assigned it."

General groaning and tsking.

Exley stops smiling. "Terry," he says, staring straight at the student. "Talk to me after class."

There is silence.

"I'll try to get these back to you by Wednesday," says Exley.

"Or Thursday," says someone.

Laughter again.

"No sense rushin' yourself."

Exley places the essays on top of his briefcase.

"Now," he says, turning around. "As promised on Friday, the comma splice."

General book shuffling and groans.

"That's pages forty-seven to fifty in the handbook."

Someone says something in the back of the room.

"And which you all," says Exley, "or most of you, seem particularly fond of constructing."

He turns and writes on the board: *John loves Mary Mary loves Alex*

He faces the room again. There is silence.

"Derrick," he says, nodding toward a student in the back of the room. "How would you punctuate this?"

Derrick looks down at his handbook.

"This sentence here, Derrick," says Exley, tapping the blackboard with chalk. "This sentence quote unquote."

"Well," says Derrick.

There is silence. Two hands go up.

Exley waits.

"Period at the end," says Derrick. "After Alex."

"Good," says Exley. He turns and places a period there. "Any place else?"

Derrick stares hard at the blackboard. Exley rearranges the papers on top of his briefcase, squaring the essays into a stack, whistling soundlessly.

Three hands are up now. Two young women in the second row start to whisper.

Derrick says nothing.

"Melinda," says Exley.

Melinda looks at her friend, at the blackboard, at Exley, then back at the blackboard.

Exley waits.

"Period after Mary," says Melinda, popping her gum. "Period after that Mary there."

"Which Mary there?"

Melinda looks at her friend. "First one," she says.

"Good," says Exley. He turns and places a period between the two Marys. "Why here, Melinda, and why not a comma?"

Three more hands go up now.

Melinda continues: "John loves Mary's a sentence."

"Good," says Exley. "Or an independent clause."

"Riiight," says Melinda.

There is laughter.

Someone else also says "Riiight."

"Right," Exley says.

He turns then and writes on the board: *John loves Mary; Mary loves Alex. Misery loves company.*

Then, just below this: *John loves Mary, but Mary loves Alex.*

"And Alex loves John," someone says.

There is laughter.

Exley looks up at the clock. It is 10:17. He turns back and circles the *but*, then the semicolon.

"What's it that makes a clause independent?" he says.

A SILVER SCIROCCO, heading east on Winnetka Avenue, comes to a stop at the intersection of Winnetka and Hibbard Road. Its left-hand turn signal is flashing.

The east-west traffic light changes from green now to yellow, and two more westbound cars proceed through the intersection. The Scirocco begins a left turn onto Hibbard. A westbound navy-blue Buick is approximately a dozen car-lengths east of the intersection, and it begins to accelerate.

Seeing the Buick, the driver of the Scirocco puts on her brakes, then apparently changes her mind and accelerates in an effort to complete the turn and get out of the way of the Buick.

The Buick keeps coming.

The driver of the Scirocco puts on the brakes again.

The Buick's driver also brakes now and swerves to his left, then begins sliding sideways into the intersection.

At this point the east-west traffic light changes from yellow to red.

The point of impact is just behind the right rear wheel of each car. The Buick, much heavier, stops almost immediately, but the force of the collision knocks the rear end of the Scirocco a foot and a half in the air and spins the car halfway around. The right rear hubcap of the Buick pops off.

The hubcap bounces three times, clanging in tremolo, then begins rolling unsteadily over the asphalt. Horns are now honking. The hubcap wobbles and tilts along an arc for twenty or twenty-five feet before it finally tips over, rotates six times on its axis, and stops.

E<small>LIZABETH'S RIGHT SHOELACE</small> is loose. She kneels on one knee, reaches down, and starts to untie it.

"Would you like me to help you with that, Elizabeth?" says Mrs. Zigulski.

"No thanks," says Elizabeth.

She crosses the two laces over themselves, lifts up the right one a little, and pushes the left one through underneath. Then she looks up and itches her nose.

Her classmates continue to yell and play instruments and paint.

She makes the right loop first and squeezes it tight at the bottom. She wraps the end of the other lace over this loop, then pushes the middle of the lace back up and through, working her loose tooth back and forth with her tongue. Now there are two loops, one big and one small.

She lets go of both of the loops and changes hands as fast as she can, grabbing the small loop with her right hand and the big loop with her left. Then she pulls both loops out till they catch.

"Now a double," she says, to herself.

She crosses the loops, guides the one on the left back down and under the right one, then pulls the knot tight.

"That's pretty good," says Mrs. Zigulski.

Elizabeth stands up and looks down at her laces. They are all right now.

"Thanks," she says. "Thanks."

A FOUR-DOOR NAVY-BLUE RABBIT waits at the stop sign at the corner of Chatfield Road and Gordon Terrace while another car goes through the intersection.

The Rabbit proceeds through the intersection and into the circular driveway at the rear of the Hubbard Woods School, pulls up next to the open gate of the playground, and stops.

There are three people inside the car: the male driver and a woman up front, another young man in the back. All three wear navy-blue stocking caps.

The motor is running.

KELLY, MACHIKO, Genevieve Rawls, and Elizabeth are the first ones in line to go out on the playground.

"What's this fuzz?" says Elizabeth.

"Fuzz?" says Machiko.

"Fuzz," says Elizabeth.

"What fuzz?" says Kelly.

"I don't see any fuzz," says Genevieve Rawls.

The four girls have opened their jackets and spread them out facing away from themselves outside down on the floor. Machiko, Elizabeth, and Genevieve have royal-blue Cubs jackets; Kelly has a navy-blue blazer with a bright red heart stitched onto one of the pockets. Now, all together, they bend over and push their hands part of the way into the sleeves, stand up a little, and—more or less simultaneously—flip the jackets back over their heads, sleeves down over their fingers, and on. They are giggling.

"I'm still hungry," says Kelly.

"Yeah, me too," say Elizabeth and Machiko, both at once.

All four say "Hey!"

Mrs. Zigulski is talking to Gordie and Jimmy.

Colin is painting.

Audrey and Mark are scaring the goldfish by tapping on the bowl with a clothespin.

Lowell is playing the glockenspiel.

Heide and John are taking turns blowing into Mrs. Zigulski's harmonica.

Mrs. Witt is helping Genevieve Webster zip up her jacket.

Carlos and Max are still drawing.

In the light through the door to the playground, Kelly's, Genevieve's, and Elizabeth's hair is light brown, the color of teak, with long streaks of blond from the summer. Machiko's hair is jet black. Machiko's, Kelly's, and Elizabeth's hair is parted in the middle and braided; all three have two braids that start near the back of their ears and reach down two or three inches past their collarbones.

"My mom just didn't have time to this morning," says Genevieve. Her hair is parted on the side and clipped back with a light blue barrette.

"How come?" says Kelly.

"I just guess we must of got up too late for her to do it," says Genevieve.

Machiko nods.

"Mine's always longer," says Kelly, "when my mom combs the braids out."

"Mine too," says Elizabeth. "My mom uses a brush."

They are measuring their hair, pulling it forward and down to see whose is longest.

"Mine too," says Kelly.

"Mine too," says Machiko.

Lowell, John, and Jimmy start to roughhouse in line now behind them.

"God," says Genevieve, rolling her eyes.

Kelly compares the length of her own braids with

Machiko's. Lowell, having been shoved, bumps into Machiko's shoulder. Machiko does not turn around.

"Watch it, you guys," says Elizabeth, looking at Jimmy. "Just stop bumping us now."

"Yeah," says Kelly. "Be careful."

Lowell laughs and says he is sorry.

"Stop that roughhousing, Jimmy," says Mrs. Witt.

"Lowell started it," says Jimmy. "He said the P-word."

"Did not!" says Lowell.

"Did too," says Jimmy.

"Well, I want both of you to stop it now," says Mrs. Witt. "Right away."

"We're *so* sorry," say Jimmy and John.

"It's okay," says Elizabeth.

"Sorry," says Lowell.

"It's okay," say Kelly and Genevieve.

"All right now," says Mrs. Zigulski. "I want all of my friends to get over in line now."

The rest of the class immediately begins to line up.

Jimmy pushes Lowell again and Lowell falls sideways and down. Jimmy laughs hard.

"Sorry, Lowell."

"Yeah," says John. "Sorry, Lowell."

Lowell pops up laughing.

"Lowell the Bowl," say Jimmy and John.

"God," says Elizabeth.

"Lowell the Hole."

"You too, Heide," says Mrs. Witt. "I want everyone to zip up those jackets."

Most of the children are over in line now.

"Are we ready?" says Mrs. Zigulski.

"Come on now, Audrey," says Mrs. Witt.

Lowell, John, and Jimmy continue to roughhouse, shoving each other into the lockers and cubbyholes, giggling. They are careful not to bump Machiko. Jimmy calls John and Lowell "dufuses."

"Let's go, Colin," says Mrs. Zigulski. "Chop chop."

Jimmy accidentally-on-purpose bumps Machiko, hard. Elizabeth exhales very loud through her nose.

The boys look away from the girls and make faces. They continue to roughhouse.

"Jimmy!" says Machiko, finally.

Shelley pulls *Harper's,* some fliers, a postcard, and two first-class bills from the mailbox and slides it all into her purse. One of the Killian's trucks is backing up into the driveway; its bumper is sporting a shiny new sticker that says PLUMBERS LAY BETTER PIPE. Shelley reads the sticker, waits for the truck to go by, then steps out onto the sidewalk.

Along with her brown leather purse, she is carrying an armful of laundry and a library book: Stravinsky's *Chroniques de ma vie.* She is wearing a Harris tweed jacket, a rolled-up pair of Jack's Levi's, and Freeds.

She stops as she passes the Chieftain Pontiac showroom and checks in her purse for her keys. They are there. Two teen-aged boys look at each other then glance at her side as they pass her.

She pauses again in front of the Hebblewaithe-Maloney Funeral Parlor and readjusts her grip on the laundry. Her straight dark brown hair is still damp.

After waiting for the light to turn green, she hurries across Tower Road. She passes the Texaco station, takes two small envelopes out of her purse, and pushes them into the mailbox.

In Zengeler's she drops the laundry on top of the counter: two woolen skirts, a dark green silk dress, Exley's navy-blue blazer and one of her own, a much smaller one of Elizabeth's, and a bundle of blue cotton shirts.

After several seconds a woman emerges from between the rows of clear plastic-covered dry cleaning. She is wearing a shiny brown wig.

"Morning," says Shelley.

The woman mumbles some greeting, glances past Shelley outside, begins thumbing through a drawerful of charge plates. "That's Exley on Green Bay . . ."

"Right."

The woman pulls out Shelley's plate, marking the place in the drawer with a Popsicle stick. "Twenty-nine thirty-three and a half."

Shelley nods.

The woman fits the plate onto the Address-O-Graph, presses the lever down, takes out the receipt, then begins counting the shirts in the bundle. Shelley takes two pieces of hard root-beer candy from the bowl on the counter. She unwraps one and puts it into her mouth; the other she drops in her purse.

The woman says "Seven."

"I guess so," says Shelley. She smiles at the woman and shrugs. "That's what he counted this morning."

The woman writes out a receipt for the shirts. "Hangers no starch?"

"Please."

After stamping it with the Address-O-Graph, the woman writes out a second receipt for the blazers, the dress, and the skirts. "Wednesday morning all right for these things?"

"Fine."

The woman puts the charge plate back in the drawer,

pulls out the Popsicle stick, hands Shelley two pink receipts.

Shelley folds them over two times, creases them sharply, puts them into her purse. "Thanks," she says. "See you Wednesday."

Outside, she uncrumples the cellophane candy wrapper, crumples it, rolls it around between her small palms while she walks.

She is sweating.

CARLOS, GORDIE, AND MAX are climbing the monkey bars. Most of the other children are either standing or racing around by the slide, trying to decide whose turn is next. Lowell is fidgeting.

Mrs. Witt is still zipping up her own jacket. Mrs. Zigulski is pushing Heide on one of the swings.

The woman in the front seat of the Rabbit points through the rear window at one of the children. The young man in back nods his head twice, pulls and twists his right earlobe, nods a third time.

The sun dazzles the face of the slide as Russell goes down it. There are no clouds or wind.

A maroon Fiat stops at the corner of Chatfield and Gordon, a half block away, then proceeds down the road past the playground.

The young man and the woman emerge from the passenger side of the Rabbit. The man leaves his door open.

Audrey and Genevieve Webster scream and shriek as Jimmy and Mark chase them around the green teetertotter.

The man and the woman stroll onto the playground, pulling the inside parts of their stocking caps down over their faces. There are holes in the front for their eyes; both have to pause for a second to get them lined up.

Mrs. Witt stops turning the jump rope and stares at the man and the woman. Mrs. Zigulski stares too.

A blackbird caws in one of the trees overhead. A second blackbird caws back.

The man starts to run toward the children. Mrs. Zigulski runs toward the man. The woman hangs back.

Most of the children stop playing. Some start to scream now. Some just stand still.

Heide is laughing.

The man grabs Elizabeth under her arms from behind and hoists her up off the ground. Mrs. Witt holds on tightly to Jimmy and Colin.

Elizabeth screams.

Mrs. Zigulski grabs the man's shoulder, but he straightens his arm, knocks her down.

Elizabeth screams.

The man readjusts his grip on Elizabeth, using both hands now. Mrs. Zigulski gets up.

The man makes a dash for the gate, trips, and falls over. He starts to get up. The woman has withdrawn a pistol from under her jacket. Raising it up with both hands, she points it at Mrs. Zigulski.

Mrs. Zigulski runs, lunges forward. She grabs ahold of the man by his forearm, slowing him down and jerking him halfway around. He still holds Elizabeth.

The woman fires the pistol three times and Mrs. Zigulski's legs shoot out from under her. One slug ricochets off the school as all three reports rocket back over the playground. Russell's hand covers his cheek; he falls over.

The woman follows Elizabeth and the man through the gate, then jumps into the Rabbit ahead of them. Elizabeth continues to scream. The man tosses Elizabeth in next to the woman, then climbs in himself, slamming the door shut behind him.

The Rabbit pulls out of the driveway and heads at a moderate speed up Gordon Terrace. The three adult occupants pull off their stocking caps.

Russell gets up on one knee, starts to cry.

The Rabbit stops at the corner and its right turn signal starts flashing. The Tower Road traffic goes by.

Children run away from and toward Mrs. Zigulski.

Some just stand still.

A HUBBARD WOODS SQUAD CAR arrives at Winnetka and Hibbard. The Scirocco still sits in the middle of the intersection, facing northeast; the Buick, flooded and stalled, is facing southwest. Cars heading south and north on Winnetka slowly make their way past them, waiting their turn then circling to the left or the right.

The driver of the Buick and the driver of the Scirocco are standing beside the Scirocco, out of the way of the traffic, examining the wheel well and bumper.

The police officer, a woman, approaches the drivers. "Anyone hurt here?" she says. "Because we've really got to get these things out of here."

"Not really," says the driver of the Buick. "It's strange, but neither of us really got hurt."

The driver of the Scirocco shakes her head twice. "I don't *think* so," she says.

Without having to be asked, the driver of the Buick hands over his driver's license.

"My *car's* kind of hurt," says the driver of the Scirocco. "Although I guess that's not quite the word."

The squad car's radio squawks insistently.

"So I can see," says the officer. She turns toward her car. "I'll be with you two in a second. In the meantime—"

Two other squad cars roar through the intersection now, lights on and sirens screaming, heading north. Gravel and smoke pour from the second car's wheel wells and both barely miss hitting the Buick.

The officer gets into her car. "Wait here," she says, pointing her finger. "Don't move from this spot but get those cars out of there."

She makes a sharp U-turn back onto Hibbard, turns on her lights and her siren, then takes off after the two other squad cars.

An enormous fireman passes Russell into the back of an ambulance. Russell is wincing and sobbing, craning his neck to see past the fireman's shoulder.

The three blocks surrounding the playground are teeming with squad cars and people. A half dozen teachers stand near the door of the school. The children have been taken inside.

Mrs. Zigulski has been placed on a stretcher. A young red-haired doctor kneels and works over her.

A huge crow caws overhead. Photographers are snapping off pictures.

Two men pick up the stretcher and carry Mrs. Zigulski toward the back of an ambulance. Her eyelids and fingers are moving.

SHELLEY STROLLS past Chieftain's showroom carrying a small bag of groceries, a gallon of milk, and her purse.

Two policemen are waiting outside her apartment. One is smoking. The other is talking to Lewis Mason, the mailman, and Johan Dini, one of the Killian's plumbers.

Shelley adjusts her grip on the groceries and looks at her watch. Then, looking ahead, she notices the rear two-thirds of the squad car that's parked in her driveway.

Dini identifies Shelley.

Shelley nods at the officers, smiles at Mason and Dini. "Mrs. Exley?"

"I'm Shelley Exley," she says. She stops five feet in front of them, readjusts her grip on the groceries. "Yes?"

"We have to speak with you, Mrs. Exley."

Shelley is silent.

"Your daughter," says one of the officers. "Elizabeth."

"Elizabeth . . ."

"Mrs. Exley . . ."

Shelley looks over at Mason, at Dini, then back at the officer. The milk carton slips from her hand.

"What?" She presses her hand to her abdomen. "What?"

Dini looks down. There's a puddle of milk by his feet.

One of the officers takes Shelley's shoulder. "May I . . . may we come in?"

Shelley shakes off his hand and backs up.

"Shelley . . ." says Dini.

Shelley stands quietly now, still holding on to the groceries.

"Tell me," she says.

TWO CAMOUFLAGE-COLORED navy helicopters, flying at an altitude of three hundred feet, crisscross the area above and around Hubbard Woods. A third flies along even lower above the northbound lanes of the Edens Expressway.

Small traffic tie-ups develop as cars begin to accumulate in back of the various roadblocks. Along Tower Road drivers wave up through their windshields, or honk, but the sound of their horns is drowned out by the noise from the chopper's propellers.

SLOWLY, ESCORTED by seven squad cars, the two ambulances make their way up Gordon Terrace. Rotating lights and sirens are on. Horns are honking. Sunlight glints hard off the chrome.

At the corner of Gordon and Tower the convoy turns right and accelerates.

"A̲ltho̲u̲gh̲ ge̲ru̲nds never are verbs," Exley says. He underlines a word on the board. "No way can they function as predicates."

Bee Cabanban, one of the English department's six secretaries, appears outside the door in the hallway.

"It just never can happen," says Exley.

Mrs. Cabanban—Exley still doesn't see her—excuses herself, raising one finger.

He sees her.

"Can I see you a minute?" she whispers.

T̲he scirocco, the Buick, their owners. Both cars have been moved to the side of the road. The owner of the Scirocco hands the owner of the Buick his hubcap.

A helicopter goes by overhead. They look up.

NOON.
The empty kitchen of the Exleys' apartment.
Three cane-backed chairs, two metal stools, a small wooden table. A green metal garbage can with a black polyethylene bag as a liner. Plain white cotton curtains tied back with nautical cord. A clock. A green plastic rack of clean dishes.

Shelley's brown leather purse lies on its side on the table. It is open.

Magnetized plastic letters in the primary colors are stuck, mostly at random, to the lower two thirds of the door of the refrigerator. A Cray-Pas drawing of a sun and a house and a girl is attached by the X and the upside down Q to the door; the Q covers part of the sun. A note on a torn piece of looseleaf is attached higher up by the R. ELIZAB TH is neatly spelled out just beneath it.

Taped to the cabinets over the oven and sink are three other drawings. One shows two frogs standing one on top of the other beside a dark purple house; the frog on the bottom is wearing a dark purple necktie. In the second, four round pink pig figures are arranged from left to right according to size: father pig, whose necktie is scarlet, and whose legs have horizontal navy-blue stripes;

mother pig, slightly shorter and rounder, in a scarlet necklace and a floor-length navy-blue dress; daughter pig, whose yellow hair is fixed with scarlet barrettes, and who wears a scarlet and green checkered shirt; and baby pig, who is naked. The third drawing shows a large peanut butter and jelly sandwich in cross section, and beside it a glass of brown milk.

Around the corner and down the short hall in the living room, someone is sobbing. A man's voice speaks softly. Other sounds, too, reach the kitchen.

A metal lighter clicks open, its flint is abraded, it closes.

A man clears his throat.

Someone coughs.

"THESE PEOPLE are really the lowest, lowest kind . . . They are scum. They don't have the balls to go out and do something like hold up a bank or, do you know what I mean? Don't have the balls to show up and try . . . I mean, these people are real fucking scum."

Two at a time, Exley runs up the stairs to his apartment. He is accompanied by a pair of detectives.

Mary Exley, his mother, leads all three men into the kitchen. "It's going to turn out all right, Jackie," she says. "How did you get here so fast?"

"Where's Shelley?"

"She's lying down now in the bedroom."

Exley and his mother embrace.

"They met me downtown at the station. I mean, she all right?"

"She's okay now," says Mary. She closes her eyes. "She was spotting, and so I—"

"About, so about how long has she known?"

"She was very shaken up at first of course. She's . . . she's upset."

Exley lets go of his mother. "Mom, this is Don Campion and Tom . . ."

"Tom Toffenetti."

"Tom Toffenetti."

Both men nod toward Mrs. Exley.

"Have you been able to find out anything else yet?"

"What we have, ma'am, so far," says Campion. "So far what we've got are those three photographs of Elizabeth, but what we still need to get hold of is that tape of her voice, the one with her talking—"

"The one—"

Mary looks up at her son. "I already called Uncle Michael."

Campion looks at the drawings.

Toffenetti continues: "We're all very confident, ma'am, that we're going to be able to locate her."

Shelley comes into the kitchen.

"Because at this point what we feel's most likely . . ."

Exley puts his arms around Shelley. He looks at his mother.

"Ma'am . . ."

Mary leads Toffenetti and Campion down the short hall toward the living room. "We'll be in here," she says. "There's another man here wants to see you."

"You okay?" Exley says.

Shelley nods.

"Because it's going to be . . ." He holds her more tightly.

Shelley just nods, shakes her head.

"Because it's all gonna turn out all right."

Dozens of cars moving in either direction jam Green Bay Road, most of the occupants staring up at the Exleys' apartment.

Seven policemen are whistling, waving their hands, shouting orders, trying to keep the cars moving.

One of the cars, its windows rolled down, has a tape deck playing "Willie the Pimp."

SHELLEY AND JACK in their bedroom.
"What I can't stop thinking about," says Shelley, "is of what they might do to her."
"I know. But I still know she's gonna be fine."
"About what they might *already* be doing."
Shelley sits down on the bed, then stands right back up as though scalded.
"I know," says Exley. "I know."
"What she's thinking about. About what she must *think*."
"Nothing," says Exley. "They're really not gonna do anything."
"And we're not there *with* her to tell her . . ."
Exley takes out a cigarette and lights it.
"You're so calm," says Shelley. "I guess that . . . that that's good."
They just stand there.
"The cops are really on top of this thing," Exley says. "Which is why I can say that I know that she's gonna be fine."
Shelley is silent.
"I promise."
"I want her home, Jack. I just want her back."

"And she'll *come* back. I promise."
"But so how can you know that?" says Shelley.
A silence.
"I keep wanting to wake up," says Shelley. "For it to be, though it sounds all, all so goddamn . . . but for me to turn out to be dreaming it."

Exley takes a drag off his cigarette then crushes it out in a small china plate on the dresser.

"Plus I've been bleeding . . ."
"Which is exactly why you should try to relax. I mean goddamn it, Shell . . ."

Using both hands, Shelley pushes her hair off her forehead.

"They already know, the police already know the car's license plate number, not to mention—"
"I know," Shelley says. She composes her face. "I know that. So what."
"I mean, how do you feel?"
They stare at each other.
"Jesus," says Shelley. They both look away. "I'm okay. I mean, Jesus." She looks at the bed. "I'll be fine."
"All the detectives they've got, radios, dogs, all the helicopters . . . You should lie down."
She ignores him.
"They're good guys," Exley says. "It's their job, things like this."
"Then did they say how something like this could've happened?"
"They've got theories, I guess. Because at this point they really don't want to start speculating."
"They don't want to speculate."
They look at each other.
"What if they ask us for money?"
"If they ask us for money—"

"I'm serious, Jack. What if they do."

"It's already all been worked out what I'll say."

"But we wouldn't have any money to *give* them."

"Plus the police are going to be—"

Shelley doubles over and winces now, clutching her abdomen. Exley takes hold of her shoulders.

"They're going to kill her," says Shelley. She can just get the words out. "I know it. I just know they're going to hurt her."

The foyer of Genevieve Rawls's house. There are fifteen white tulips in a vase on a small antique table. Beside them are two unlit candles, an ashtray, some letters, a newspaper, and two magazines. A carpeted staircase leads up and around to the left from the dark gray slate floor. Prokofiev's Second Sonata is playing somewhere upstairs.

To the right of the foyer, speaking into the telephone, is Genevieve's dad, Burke Rawls, Jr. He stands on the second of the four slate steps that lead down into the living room. He is tall. The person on the other end of the line is doing most of the talking.

He loosens his tie now and steps down into the living room.

He grimaces, nods. "Unforeseeable."

The living room is thirty by forty-five feet, with a fifteen-foot ceiling. On one of the long walls, framed in unfinished oak, is a hard-focused, mostly white canvas: *Pitcher and Cups with White Stripes* by Jeanette Pasin Sloan. Opposite and framed much more ornately, on the wall to the left of the fireplace, is Seurat's *An Afternoon at La Grande Jatte (A Study)*.

Anne Rawls, wearing a dark green terrycloth warm-up suit, comes into the room now, dangling two cans of Pepsi still held together by white plastic rings, and a drink.

"Gotta go now," says Rawls. "But you do that . . . right. And you tell them—"

Genevieve dashes into the room now past her mother and jumps into her father's left arm.

"Whichever," says Rawls. He transfers his daughter from his left to right arm, then kisses her cheek. "I'll talk to these guys."

"Daddy, guess what."

"Right," says Rawls. "The two-o'clock people . . . tomorrow. Okay . . . fine . . . bye." He hangs up the phone.

"Guess what happened at my school today, Daddy."

"I heard, honey," says Rawls. He looks at his wife.

"That's because you came home so early, right? From your work?"

Rawls holds Genevieve's cheek in his hand and says yes.

"And Luz made some cookies for us."

"She did?"

"Yup. And some man shot Mrs. Zigulski."

Anne takes a sip of her drink, then another. "Veevee, Daddy already—"

"That's why I came home so early," says Rawls. He lowers Genevieve onto the couch, sits down beside her, snaps open one of the Pepsis. "I heard what happened at your school today, and that's why I came home so early."

A BOX-SHAPED orange and white van—an ambulance—is parked in the Killian's driveway. A dozen reporters, three Hubbard Woods policemen, and a minicam crew from NewsCenter5 are standing close by.

The minicam operator steps forward into the doorway, focusing, then begins to back up and shoot as Shelley is brought out the door on a stretcher. Other reporters surge forward, shouting, taking pictures. Campion and Exley ignore them.

Two attendants slide the stretcher into the back of the ambulance. A third holds the door.

Campion says something to Exley. Exley leans in and says something to Shelley but does not get into the ambulance with her. He hands the paramedic her purse.

Exley says something to one of the reporters—a middle-aged woman, tall, wearing sunglasses—but Campion takes him by the shoulder and leads him back toward the doorway.

Exley turns.

The siren goes on, a policeman on Green Bay signals that it's now safe to turn, and the ambulance pulls out of the driveway.

"AND I'M SERIOUS, man. I am deadly deadly serious now. Because there's simply no way to determine that. The entire business is steeped just too deep in the shit, the upshot being that out of the blue now here comes this second fucker, you know, out of nowhere. . . . Do you know what I mean?"

Exley takes three small green oranges out of the refrigerator and starts slicing them in half on the counter top. "I can't think."

He takes a blue plastic juice squeezer down from the cupboard and fits it over the top of a mug. Then he stops.

His mother looks up.

"I can't even think."

He fits an orange half on top of the squeezer then presses and twists it; a clear stream of juice trickles down into the mug. He dumps the half rind and the pulp in the garbage, replaces the squeezer on top of the mug and fits on another half orange, starts pressing and twisting again; the juice trickles down.

The mug shoots out now from under the squeezer and skitters against the back of the counter. It spins there for a second then stops, still intact.

"Jackie," says Mary. "Glory be . . ."

Exley grabs the mug, cocks his arm, looks for a safe place to throw it.

He puts it back down on the counter.

The telephone rings.

There is silence.

By the second ring Toffenetti has appeared in the kitchen. He looks hard at Exley. "You ready?"

Exley nods.

The telephone rings. Toffenetti turns on a cassette deck. "Okay."

Exley picks up the receiver just as the fourth ring is starting. "Hello?"

He closes his eyes, turns, shakes his head.

Mary goes to the counter now and starts to clean up the pulp.

"Right," Exley says. "You heard right. That's . . . yes. Listen, Natalie . . . right. And I know you'll understand if we've really got to keep this line open."

Toffenetti turns off the deck and goes out.

"Sure," Exley says. "We'll talk to you later. She'll . . . of course . . . Right." He hangs up.

"Goddamn fucking Natalie," he says, to himself.

A ROOM WITH white walls.
Sneakers across a tile floor.
That, and some voices.

"What I really want to do now is pray," Exley says. "Just get down on my knees and beg, you know, for her to come back to us safe."

"She will," says his mother. "I know it."

Exley sits down.

"That's what we're all praying for, even Shelley, and *for* Shelley too. And it's going to happen."

"I've been *trying* to pray, doing something, that that will happen." He shakes his head, coughs. "There's no way I can."

"There's no one who can't pray, Jackie. Especially in a situation like this."

"Yeah, that's just it, though. I've never really prayed for anything before. I mean, nothing. So why should God want to put up with it now?"

"That's silly," says Mary. "That's simply not true."

"Because what I'm trying to do, I suppose, is make praying make some sort of sense to me now. And it doesn't."

"God doesn't 'put up' with things we do or not put up with them. He just, He's just there."

"Yeah, there. He's just there, or up there, we're down here . . . and he's over there at the school this morning—"

"All I know is, if you prayed to Him now, God would answer you."

"He would, would He."

"Even if it's the first time you've prayed in your life."

Exley lights a cigarette from the one he is smoking.

"Believe me, Jackie."

"My believing you's not the point, Mom. Try and understand that. I haven't believed in God, things like praying, for what? twenty years? Since I was an altar boy back in grammar school."

"Well?"

"Since I was Elizabeth's age."

"Well?"

"Well, so it would be a bit opportunistic, wouldn't you say, to start again now."

"It would hardly—"

"I mean, a little bit too much of a coincidence? Now, all of a sudden like that?"

"No, I don't, Jackie."

"It would be a classic case of bad faith, Mom. It would just be really bad faith."

"All you're telling me is that you're *afraid* to pray now."

"Listen, Mom. Listen. There's good faith and there's bad faith. The kind I've got now's very bad."

They are silent.

"Being unsure about what you should do is, it's all part of faith, part of praying. If you were sure about certain things you'd never have need—"

"I'm afraid I can't follow that logic, Mom. No offense."

"There's nothing—"

"Right, right. I know. There's nothing logical about it."

They are silent.

"I'm trying now, Mom. Whatever I say, I am trying."

"You couldn't cheat God, Jackie. You couldn't."

They are silent.

"Okay," says Exley. "Here goes, then." He presses his hands together and looks at the ceiling. "Okay?"

His mother looks down.

"Dear God," Exley says. "Please make everything better now. Please just make it all better. Please bring Elizabeth—"

"Not that way, Jackie," says Mary. She stands up and goes to him. "That isn't the way."

"It isn't, huh."

"No, it's not."

Fifteen seconds go by. They neither look at nor speak to each other. Thirty seconds.

At last Exley says, "What's the way?"

THE RAWLSES' FRONT DOORBELL chimes and Luz Cordova-Valez, their maid, goes to answer it.

The man at the door—he is bearded, with very long hair—is from the Hubbard Woods Post Office. He hands Luz an envelope. "Special delivery, ma'am."

Luz takes the envelope, thanks him, closes the door.

Anne Rawls comes into the living room. "Who was that?"

"Letter," says Luz. "Special delivery." She examines the envelope briefly, then hands it to Anne. "For Mr. Rawls."

Anne takes the envelope and, weighing it and looking it over, carries it into the study. Rawls is inside at his desk, writing on a large yellow pad.

"Special delivery," says Anne. She hands him the envelope. "No return address . . ."

Rawls thanks her, takes a pair of scissors out of his drawer, cuts off the end of the envelope.

"Who's it from?"

"Haven't the foggiest, dear," says Rawls. He looks up at Anne, begins to say something else to her, doesn't.

He pulls a single sheet of white bond typing paper out of the envelope, opens it, reads:

1. *We make no mistakes. Our errors are volitional and are the portals of discovery. So don't fuck with us.*
2. *We have Elizabeth Exley instead of your daughter. Elizabeth will be returned in one piece to her nuclear family if and only if you, Burke Rawls, Esq., deliver to us three hundred carats of D-E, VVS, diamonds. No diamond should be smaller than three carats or larger than five.*
3. *You have until 5:00 P.M. Tuesday—one business day—to gather together these diamonds. This deadline will not be extended.*
4. *If you claim to have insufficient funds to meet this demand, you're a liar. Talk to your friends at Commonwealth Edison and or the Illinois Arts Council. Or think of it as one more campaign contribution. Or talk to your wife.*
5. *If you claim that you aren't responsible for the life of Elizabeth Exley, you are also a liar. The systemic violence of you and your ilk has been contributing all along to her slow-motion murder. Our action today merely underscores this hideous fact; it is the necessary counterviolence that is called for. The labor we delight in physics pain.*
6. *It's the old carat-or-stick routine, Burke. You of all people should understand how it works: either we get the diamonds or Elizabeth here gets the stick. Or think of it as the law of supply and demand: Right now Elizabeth's in real short supply, our demands are above. Dot dot dot.*
7. *This will be our final contact with you until the deadline on Tuesday. Do meet it. There will be no negotiations. There will be no explanations. There will be no C.O.D.'s. There will be no waiting around on your part or ours. There will be no guarantees. That you will pay up on time and in full is all that will happen.*
8. *That we are serious about this should have already been demonstrated outside the Hubbard Woods School. If there is any delay whatsoever, any last-minute "mix-up," any short-*

age of carats or quality, or any outside interference at all, it will be our duty to kill young Elizabeth. You can count on it.

By now Rawls is standing, holding the letter in one hand, the envelope in the other.

"Honey?" says Anne. It's the third time she's spoken.

Rawls now pulls a Polaroid photograph from inside the envelope. It's a picture, in color, of Elizabeth Exley, wearing her Cubs jacket, sitting in what appears to be a canvas director's chair, looking scared.

Rawls begins to hand the letter over to Anne, then pulls back his hand and starts reading again.

"Burke, what is it?"

Rawls stares down at the photograph. He is silent.

"Who's it from?"

Luz appears in the doorway now, holding a carton of ice cream.

"Jesus, Burke."

Rawls hands Anne the letter, continues to stare at the Polaroid. "Where's Veevee?" he says.

EXLEY HANGS UP the telephone.
"Well?"
He is silent.
"What did they say?"
"I guess she's asleep now."
"That's the best thing for her, Jackie. That's good."
"They've got her on some sort of sedative . . . some very mild sedative, and something for the 'incompetent cervix.'"
"She'll be fine."
"And they've got one of those intrauterine monitors . . ."
"She's going to be fine. I just know it."
They are silent.
"Jesus," says Exley. He massages his eyes with his palms. "I really can see, I mean how . . ."
They are silent.
"You know what she told me before the ambulance came? That she was going to kill herself if Elizabeth wasn't okay."
"Elizabeth, Jackie, is gonna come back, and Shelley wouldn't *do* something like that."
Exley sits down at the table.
"She wouldn't be able to, with the doctors and all. And you know that. But that's not the point. She just wouldn't want to. She's upset. She was only upset."

They are silent.

"Jackie, listen. What I was just saying, when Timothy died, you were still too young to remember this, I held him for five or six hours, his body. I couldn't see how anything else in the world could've mattered. I just sat there in bed for six hours, holding onto him."

"But you got over it."

"We all did. He was dead. We got over it when your father died too."

"Wonderful, Mom. Only what if we don't get to hold onto Elizabeth for the requisite number of hours?"

"Jackie . . ."

"Oh, so the point must be that if Elizabeth doesn't come back, Shelley will somehow get over it, so that therefore don't worry?"

"It's nothing like that. What you'll get over, what both of you will get over is, is the thing that she's gone now. Temporarily."

"Temporarily."

"Only temporarily, Jackie. I'm certain of it. Just for a while."

Exley looks out the window.

"I can *feel* it, Jackie. I know it."

They are silent.

"What else did they say?"

"What? The cops?"

"The hospital."

"Shit. Nothing."

"Nothing about how—"

"The hospital said nothing. The cops have said nothing. Does that . . . does that answer your question? And we're sitting here now in the kitchen here, talking about . . ."

They are silent.

F̲BI HEADQUARTERS, Department of Justice, D.C. The following print-out slides neatly, folding itself at thirteen-inch intervals, into a dark gray metal receptacle:

EVENT: EXLEY/RAWLS
TYPE: KIDNAPPING
DATE: 1006
LOCATION: HUBBARD WOODS HIGH SCHOOL
LOCALE: HUBBARD WOODS IL
REGION: MIDWEST
HOST-COUNTRY: N/A
ANNOUNCED-CLAIMANT:
WHEN-CLAIMED: 1635
ANNOUNCED-PURPOSE:
DISCLAIMANT:
TARGET: GENEVIEVE RAWLS
TARGET-SYMBOLIC-VALUE:
TARGET-ACCESSIBILITY: HIGH
VICTIM: ELIZABETH EXLEY
BOMB-WEIGHT: 5 OZ
BOMB-TYPE: AUTOMOBILE
BOMB-SIZE: SMALL
BOMB-DELIVERY: PLANTED
BOMB-DETONATION: REMOTE (COMMAND RADIO)

SECONDARY-DETONATION: NO DETONATION
DETONATION-SOURCE: PERPETRATOR
BOMB-COMPOSITION: PLASTIQUE
EXPLOSIVE-SOURCE: COMMERCIAL
BOMB-SOPHISTICATION: MEDIUM
AUDACITY: MEDIUM
RISK-TO-PERPETRATOR: LOW
RECIPIENT-OF-WARNING: NO WARNING
WARNING-TIME: NO WARNING TIME
OUTCOME: DETONATED
TACTICAL-OBJECTIVE: EXTORTION
STRATEGIC-OBJECTIVE: DISTRACTION
NUMBER-KILLED: 0
NUMBER-WOUNDED: 0
PRIMARY-DAMAGE: LOW
SECONDARY-DAMAGE: NO DAMAGE
INSTIGATOR:
PERPETRATOR:
GROUP-NAME:
POLITICAL-IDEOLOGY:
NATIONALITY: AMERICAN
AGE:
OBJECTIVE: KIDNAPPING FOR RANSOM
ACTION-FREQUENCY:
PAST-INCIDENTS:
AFFILIATIONS: NO AFFILIATIONS CLAIMED
STAGES-OF-DEVELOPMENT:
ETHNIC-COMPOSITION: WHITE
EDUCATIONAL-COMPOSITION: UNIVERSITY
SUPPORTERS: NO SUPPORTERS
LEVEL-OF-SOPHISTICATION: MEDIUM
TACTICS: BOMBING, KIDNAPPING, ASSAULT
TYPE: ARMED
ACTIVITY-SPAN:

TARGETS: GENEVIEVE RAWLS
MEMBERS: 3 OR MORE
HEADQUARTERS-LOCATION:
TERRITORY-OF-OPERATIONS:
LEVEL-OF-SUPPORT: INSIGNIFICANT
TYPE-OF-SUPPORT: INSIGNIFICANT

A blue-suited man with an eye-patch waits for the print-out to finish, tears off the paper, then carries it down a long corridor.

"And I couldn't sleep *at all* the night she was finally born."

"I remember that day."

"I had dinner over at your house. Had to leave both of them down there at the hospital."

"We had lasagna."

"Right." Exley nods. "That's right. The lasagna. But what I couldn't help thinking about when I finally got into bed was all the things that might've gone wrong. Born with no arms, mongoloid, blind, retarded . . . things like that. That we all of a sudden had this perfectly normal healthy baby on our hands didn't seem to make those other possibilities even *slightly* less scary. Didn't even seem to make them less possible."

His mother is silent.

"It was a matter . . ." He lights a cigarette. "It was almost as though . . ."

They are silent.

"And the whole time Shelley was pregnant that time, I mean I really wanted it to be a boy. But then as soon as E-beth came out and they wrapped her up and passed her on over to me . . ." He snaps his fingers. "Couldn't've mattered less."

"Of course not."

"Anyway, but the other thing I kept thinking about was what *still* might go wrong, all the problems I wanted her never to have to put up with."

"And probably all the same things your father and I didn't want you and Tim to have to face either."

"Getting hit by cars, plane crashes, acne, hassles with boys or at school, leukemia."

"Acne and leukemia?"

"Anything and everything," says Exley. "Anything bad. I just didn't want it to happen to *her*. I always wanted to, to be able to keep it from happening."

His mother is silent.

"And so but of all the things I'd imagined . . ." Exley is sobbing now, trying to stop himself, rubbing his eyes with his forearm. "I could never . . . because I never thought something like this, *this,* could have *happened.*"

WHAT WE HAVE THEN is less than the proverbial twenty-four hours."

"Not even—"

"One business day."

"Jesus."

"We've got enough time."

"Not even till sundown."

There are nine people sitting in Burke Rawls's study: Alex Brett, Gerry Albers, and James Andrewjewski, FBI special agents from the Special Operations and Research unit based in downtown Chicago; Sidney Ruth, senior financial officer of NorthCentral Industries; Frank Finn, Hubbard Woods chief of police; Sandra Lennon, North-Central's senior legal counsel; Herbert Dundee, North-Central's public relations officer; and the Rawlses. Introductions have already been made, extra chairs have been brought down from the guest rooms, and copies of the eight-point ransom letter have been distributed.

"Plus or minus, oh—"

"Only a very small part of this stuff can be verified."

A reel-to-reel tape recorder sits on a chair just to the right of Rawls's large desk; someone has laid a clip-board on top of it. A smaller cassette deck is being examined by Albers.

"It's *all* kind of borderline, actually."

"More or less."

"It's ticklish ticklish business."

Two walls of the study are lined, floor to ceiling, with bookshelves. On a third wall are three framed black-and-white photographs, three framed certificates, and a small oil portrait of a girl with red hair, by Cassatt.

Luz appears in the doorway, sniffs, disappears.

A blackboard and corkboard, both empty, both four feet by six feet, stand side by side in front of the room's single window, blocking the lower three fifths of its view. It has just gotten dark out.

Anne Rawls gets up, turns around, and looks out the door, then sits down again. She takes a sip of her drink.

"We've got another set of headphones and a copying machine out in our van," says Albers. "It's out in the driveway."

Two Illinois Bell technicians, in the process of hooking up six extra telephones, move—businesslike, unobtrusive—in and out of the study.

"We should start looking at that right away," says Lennon. "Have the parents been contacted yet?"

"The mother is pregnant," says Anne. Her fingers are trembling. "I think . . . I think that we know her."

"I don't think so," says Rawls.

"Not yet," says Andrewjewski.

"They took her down to the emergency room," says Finn. "At Evanston. We advised Mr. Exley to stay put for a while in his apartment. You know, for the call."

"For the time being," says Brett.

"Right."

Anne massages her neck, sips her drink.

"It's probably necessary—"

"Looks like the old difficulty switch just got turned up."

"It is necessary that we have the absolute cooperation, that even those persons on the periphery, the television people . . ."

"Exactly."

"It's not the sort of thing you can quash simply by snapping your fingers."

Luz reappears now, excusing herself, carrying a neat stack of five large porcelain ashtrays. "That icemaker's broken all weekend," she says. "No have . . . we have no ice at all."

"No ice at all," someone says.

"Really."

There is laughter.

"We've got no ice at all."

"Your hands are tied, our hands are tied, and these people take out really anybody they want to these days. Just out walking along on the sidewalk, or out in a crowd, say, driving along, he's even guarded or something . . . It's not a big deal for these people. And they pick off your *kid* fucking no sweat at all. Picking off, you know, somebody's kid's even *less* of a problem. It's really no problem at all."

B‍URKE RAWLS calls Exley.

He explains what has happened, apologizes, promises Exley that everything humanly possible will be done to bring back his daughter.

Exley tells Rawls he does not own a car. It is agreed that an agent will leave right away to pick Exley up and drive him back over to Rawls's.

Exley thanks Rawls for calling.

BERNIE ZIGULSKI, Dr. Francis Mariner, and Special Agent Frank Schuster, all three sitting bolt upright, all silent, in Dr. Mariner's office.

"I want to be straight with you, Mr. Zigulski," says Mariner, finally. "Mrs. Zigulski's condition is, isn't good. Which is why we took her back down to the OR."

Zigulski says nothing.

"The procedure I told you about is a fairly complicated procedure. We expect she'll be down there another five or six hours. We've got a couple of the very best—"

"When I saw her before . . ."

"The femoral artery, the artery that supplies most of the blood to that leg, plus the other wound—"

"We're going to find these people, Mr. Zigulski," says Schuster. "Your wife is a very brave woman."

"I don't want to hold out any false hope to you, either," says Mariner.

"Please," says Zigulski, shaking his head.

"We would never—"

"And we'll keep you informed on how she is doing as we proceed. As of now . . ."

"I want you to find these people."

"We will," says Schuster, now standing. "I'm on my way out to check up on that now."

"I want you to save her."

"We will, Mr. Zigulski," says Mariner. "We're working on that very hard."

EXLEY: And I understand that.
LENNON: And Mr. Rawls understands how it is that, because any person in your situation would certainly insist—
EXLEY: I've got no alternative.
RAWLS: And we can all understand that.
ANDREWJEWSKI: We do sympathize with your position on this, Mr. Exley.
EXLEY: But I don't see how *you've* got any alternative, either. That's my whole point.
RAWLS: It has never been a question, since I first got word from these people, of whether or not ... To be perfectly frank, Jack, I'd insist too.
EXLEY: Not to mention your unsurpassed zeal in getting in touch with me.
Silence.
ANDREWJEWSKI: And Mr. Rawls has implicitly agreed with this principle. He's felt that way from the outset.
RAWLS: Not for one moment—
EXLEY: Okay. Fine. But so if *you* don't have it, who does?
LENNON: And as Mr. Andrewjewski has pointed out, there are a number of ways—
EXLEY: Now hold it.

RAWLS: There's only one way really, of course. What we all have to do is get together and arrange for, to make it happen. How much or who has it has never been the question for us.

EXLEY: One single way. *However* you manage to get it arranged.

LENNON: You've already seen the figures, though, Jack. That's the bottom line, as they say, all the shares. There's really nothing that the Rawls family, NorthCentral Industries, rumors about the size of the Jaffe estate notwithstanding, that you haven't been privy to here.

RAWLS: We're certainly not trying to hide anything.

EXLEY: And as *I* have already stated, I have no real choice but to believe you.

LENNON: I mean, you *have* seen the figures.

EXLEY: But that's not the point. Who's got the money in which set of accounts, as far as I'm concerned, that's wholly beside the point.

ANDREWJEWSKI: And yet it's a factor that *does* enter into—

RAWLS: The point's that we've got to get Jack's daughter home safely, and we're going to do that.

EXLEY: Exactly.

Silence.

ANDREWJEWSKI: We know how to handle these things, Mr. Exley.

Long silence.

EXLEY: What I can't understand, you know, what I can't figure out is how they've assumed you'd be able to come up with, with it all. They've obviously scoped this whole thing out pretty carefully.

ANDREWJEWSKI: In the first place, Jack, they've already demonstrated quite clearly that they *can* make mistakes.

Silence.

RAWLS: I mean, with the kind of money we're talking about—
LENNON: We really don't know. We can't say. But there isn't. There just isn't.
EXLEY: Somewhere, Mrs. Lennon, there is.
LENNON: The real evidence is in front of us here on the table. We can't speak for terrorists or whatever cockeyed inferences they've made from some—
EXLEY: Then it looks like *I'm* the one who's gonna have to speak for them here, Mrs. Lennon.
Silence.
ANDREWJEWSKI: They have already spoken, Jack. For themselves. It's up to us now to respond, for us to all get together here on an effective response and—
EXLEY: Right. Sure. But it's still Mr. Rawls, is it not, who determines the nature of that response. Mr. Rawls and his lawyers—
ANDREWJEWSKI: Not really. No.
EXLEY: I mean they've got control, or whatever, of the Jaffe estate. All that money's controlled by—
LENNON: What these people have done is attacked, they've been insidiously unfair to Burke here *as well as* to you. The irony is that neither of you, that both of you, are totally innocent of any wrongdoing whatever, of doing—
EXLEY: Don't talk to me about ironical, Mrs. Lennon. Just don't. Don't make me laugh.
ANDREWJEWSKI: Jack, listen—
EXLEY: Because it's hardly the same situation. If you thought about that for a minute, you'd see that.
Silence.
RAWLS: It could just as easily—
EXLEY: Yeah, but it didn't. And there's nothing even *remotely* ironical—

LENNON: Believe me I have, Mr. Exley. All this evening I have. Quite a lot.

EXLEY: I'll bet you have, Mrs. Lennon.

Silence.

ANDREWJEWSKI: And there is still an excellent chance that Mr. Rawls, the admittedly rather slippery accounting difficulties aside, will be able to come up with a sufficient amount.

EXLEY: So please don't give me any of these fey little connotations about fairness or irony, Mrs. Lennon. Not in the situation my daughter's in. Don't.

ANDREWJEWSKI: Okay. I think—

EXLEY: Just don't.

ANDREWJEWSKI: I think Jack's made his point. I agree with you. I also agree with Mr. Rawls that despite, that there's an excellent excellent chance that the funds can be gathered together.

RAWLS: They can be.

EXLEY: When.

Silence.

RAWLS: If, by tomorrow . . . all indications so far from Manhattan are that we'll be able to manage it. That's the important, the important thing, Jack, is that—

EXLEY: By when.

RAWLS: At the very latest, by noon tomorrow.

Silence.

EXLEY: Noon.

A̲NNE RAWLS AND TERESA O'DONNELL, her sister, on the Rawlses' screened-in back patio. Through the darkness, 125 yards beyond them: Lake Michigan. Three Cook County sheriffs accompanied by two German shepherds are patrolling the grounds in between.

"What a weird weird situation this is," says Teresa. "You know, here in this town?"

"It's incredible."

"It was inevitable, I guess."

"It's so . . . disorienting."

The two women are drinking vodka martinis, eating wheat crackers, and smoking.

"You told Daddy yet?" says Teresa.

"He'd already heard it from Pat. I just guess Pat must've called him."

"What's Burke gonna do, do you think?"

"I don't know. He's very, you know. Says he'll handle it."

"But of course."

"He really doesn't have a whole hell of a lot of choice, though."

"Have you . . ." Teresa leans back in her chair and looks toward the lake. "You know, signed anything?"

They are silent.

"I mean, I can't think of anything worse you could do to a person," says Anne. "It's just really . . . your *child*."

"Probably neither could they."

"That's exactly what Burke said."

"There isn't."

"Because it could have been Genevieve. That's the thing . . . That's the thing *I* can't get over."

"Or Jeannie or Jason, for that matter."

"I mean, it practically was."

"But it wasn't, Annie. It wasn't."

"It's just such a mean shitty thing to have done."

They are silent.

"And they still can't decide in there about whether or not to show the girl's father that letter."

Teresa puts out her cigarette.

"Because I don't know *what* I'd be doing right now if it would've been Veevee."

"There's not much you'd be able *to* do, really. Although not anything all that much different, I guess."

"I guess not," says Anne. "I don't know."

ANDREWJEWSKI: Plus or minus.

EXLEY: Because another problem I've got is with there being some sort of plan, you know, in which one of your agents tries to recover the money, the diamonds, while the transfer's being made.

ANDREWJEWSKI: I can see—

EXLEY: Behind my back, as it were.

ANDREWJEWSKI: There is no such plan, Jack, and it would be better, really be better for all of us now if we sat—

EXLEY: Yeah. But you say, yet you say . . . Say that you did get some sort of fix on where they're at, where they're headed. What happens then?

LENNON: Because—

RAWLS: Because you think it might endanger Elizabeth.

EXLEY: You got it.

ANDREWJEWSKI: Our number-one priority throughout this operation is going to be your daughter's own personal safety. That's official Justice Department policy and that's Mr. Rawls's personal policy.

EXLEY: Yeah.

ANDREWJEWSKI: Only there's—

EXLEY: And yet, what if you *did* get a fix on them? What if you do? Say, tonight. What are the second, third, the fifteenth priorities?

ANDREWJEWSKI: If that happens, Jack—

RAWLS: We don't want to spook them, of course.

ANDREWJEWSKI: And you definitely will have your input, Jack. And it will be major. Believe me.

Silence.

ANDREWJEWSKI: It's very much part of the game plan.

Silence.

RAWLS: I've been trying to put myself in your shoes all along, Jack. As has Anne.

LENNON: We all have.

EXLEY: You've certainly put *me* into them, into these shoes.

RAWLS: All I'm saying is that—

EXLEY: Put Elizabeth into them . . .

ANDREWJEWSKI: I'd say we've all been put into this one together. Which is why—

EXLEY: Shit. Very true. But in all honesty . . . very true up to a point. But in all honesty, you'll have to admit that there *is* a good case to be made, I mean—

LENNON: That Mr. Rawls and his family were in no way responsible for your daughter's being kidnapped this morning?

RAWLS: Although I'm sure Sandy's point—

EXLEY: Just that it isn't, that getting her back might not be entirely the Rawlses' . . . liability. And so if you're thinking along those lines at all, I'd like to know about it.

RAWLS: We're not, Jack.

ANDREWJEWSKI: We're not.

RAWLS: None of us caused this. Neither one of us.

Silence.

ANDREWJEWSKI: We've been through this before, Jack.

RAWLS: And I fully intend to keep my promise to you and your daughter. I'm still very anxious to.
EXLEY: If you can.
RAWLS: If I can.
Silence.
ANDREWJEWSKI: There's always a certain amount of . . . volatility in situations like these. I think we all realize that.
Silence.
EXLEY: I just want to make certain.
LENNON: That we'll be able to pay the whole figure?
EXLEY: That you *will* pay them off. That you *will*. The whole fucking figure, as you call it.
ANDREWJEWSKI: Mr. Exley . . .
RAWLS: And yet that's all that I *can* do, Jack. What I can.
EXLEY: Meaning what?
RAWLS: Meaning that there are certain lengths to which everyone is prepared to go—you, me, Mr. Andrewjewski, the kidnappers, the insurance company . . .
LENNON: The only problem's that it's hard to tell just what they are.
RAWLS: At this stage, in fact, it's impossible.
ANDREWJEWSKI: It's a ticklish situation we're in, Jack.
EXLEY: I know that.
LENNON: And so simply repeating ourselves isn't going to accomplish—
ANDREWJEWSKI: What you've got to keep in mind, Jack, is that to this point we've had no assurances whatever that *they're* going to play fair with *us*.
RAWLS: I mean, we're in here, they're out there, and—
ANDREWJEWSKI: And what goes down isn't always commutative.
EXLEY: Just what does that mean? What that means is that whether they're gonna get paid's still very much up in the air. That after all this talk, after my wife—

RAWLS: No, Jack. It doesn't. Just listen.
ANDREWJEWSKI: Just listen.
RAWLS: And what's fair in a situation like this really has nothing to do with it. Somehow we're going to pay them, on time, and that's it.
Long silence.
EXLEY: I know I seem frantic—I mean, I must really be—
ANDREWJEWSKI: It's just that our assuming they're going to behave certain ways by no means guarantees it.
Long silence.
EXLEY: Let me say this, Mr. Rawls. I'm more than a little screwed up now, a little confused. But so far this evening you've given me fairly good reason to trust you, to believe you have my daughter's best interests in mind.
RAWLS: I have, Jack. I do.
EXLEY: I mean, this is a shitty spot to be in for both of us.
RAWLS: And I'm sure that in my position you'd do the same.
EXLEY: What you've got to understand, what I want is for the situation to be such that it is *altogether impossible* that my daughter will not return safely. Period. Good odds don't mean shit to me now. Because as far as I'm concerned, it's no longer a question of your being reasonable or unreasonable, or generous, or of your acting honorably or dishonorably or fairly. I just want my child back.
RAWLS: We all want her back, Jack.
ANDREWJEWSKI: We do.
LENNON: We all do.
Silence.
EXLEY: Okay.
Silence.

RAWLS: And I want you to trust me. I would never— what I mean is, we'll all be—

ANDREWJEWSKI: We *will* get her back, Jack.

Silence.

EXLEY: Then what I want right now is your word that there is *absolutely no way* you can fail to deliver to them what they want, no matter what, no matter what happens, and that she will be brought back by tomorrow.

LENNON: You have his word.

INSIDE THE SAFE HOUSE. A black-and-white television on a beige Formica counter, pushed up against a white wall. "Monday Night Football" is on.

The camera pans the crowd and the Honey Bears, and Howard Cosell gives the score: Chicago Bears 23, Tampa Bay Buccaneers 0.

Bear kicker Bob Thomas tees up the ball on his thirty-five-yard line, then backs up and raises his hand. The wind blows the ball off the tee.

Frank Gifford notes what has happened. Someone—female, unseen—sighs in disgust at the action.

Bob Thomas tees up the ball and backs up.

"When this Bear front four gets a lead now," says Fran Tarkenton, "they can really put their ears back and come."

The wind blows the ball off the tee. Someone snorts.

"Plank's been coming, Fencik's been coming . . ."

"Four sacks already this evening," says Gifford, "nineteen so far on the season."

Cosell laughs as Bob Thomas prepares once again to kick off. "Moreover, Giff, Mike Ditka, ever volatile . . ."

The picture now cuts to Mike Ditka, then quickly to one

of the Honey Bears; hands on her hips, she grins at the camera and kicks.

Bob Thomas finally manages to kick the ball off. It rises and carries end over end to the ten. A wedge of Buc blockers forms to the right, but Doug Plank knifes through it and tackles the ball carrier on his own seventeen. Someone whoops. Someone claps. Someone whistles.

"I thought you didn't like these Bears, Howard," says Tarkenton. Tarkenton and Gifford start laughing.

"Frannie, I *never* said that," says Cosell. "At no point have I ever put forward that sentiment."

Tampa Bay huddles.

"Doug Williams's work's been cut out for him," says Gifford.

A hand reaches out, changes channels.

"The news been on yet?"

"Get the Series."

Channel 5. Don Sutton delivers a change-up; Ozzie Smith, fooled, swings and misses.

"Velocity and location," says Tom Seaver. Don Sutton spits. "As someone once noted, the matrix mechanics of pitching."

"Hey, where's the Bears?"

Sutton looks in for the sign.

"Tom Terrific."

R<small>OOM</small> 3133, Obstetrics and Gynecology Ward, Evanston Community Hospital.

Exley leans forward, head in his hands, on a chair alongside Shelley's bed. Shelley is wearing a robe and pajamas, an IV line leads out one of the sleeves to an upside-down bottle half full of transparent liquid. Her records and chart are clipped to a board on the bedstead.

"At least," Exley says, looking up. "At least it's begun to make some sort of sense."

They begin to hold hands.

"Whatever that means."

Shelley stays silent. Their hands fall away from each other.

"And that you might start to, now, maybe feel better."

Shelley is silent.

"How do you feel?"

"I'm okay. Traisman says I have to, because of the cervix, relax."

Again, they hold hands.

"You've got to force yourself to," Exley says. "Really concentrate hard on it. The Rawlses are going to take—"

"You just got through saying it was too early to tell yet. That even the—"

"What I meant was, it wasn't real clear yet which set of accounts would, you know, it was going to come from."

"So the money part's settled?"

"They sound pretty positive. The important thing is that they do have the money and that they're willing to pay it."

"And so it's definite then."

"Far's I can tell . . ."

Shelley takes back her hand now and dries off her palm on the sheet. "So both of the Rawlses agree that it's their responsibility too?"

"It's *all* theirs, honey. They know that. Burke Rawls . . . I mean, he gave me his word several times."

They are silent.

"I've been doing some of those Lamaze exercises to try to relax."

Exley nods. "And Traisman's been telling me, and I told him to be straight with me, to be as objective as possible. He told me you're gonna be fine. So's the baby."

"Maybe that way I won't have to take as strong a sedative."

They are silent.

"It's really a pretty clear-cut situation," says Exley. "At least now we know—"

Shelley inhales jaggedly now through her mouth. "Though I guess, I guess what happened wasn't really their fault."

"They're good people, Shell. I mean, in a way we've been lucky so far, as far as that goes."

"It's just that—"

"And I know it's a strange thing to say now, but I really don't think we have all that much to worry about anymore."

Quietly, closing her eyes, Shelley cries.

Exley holds on to her hand. "I'm serious, Shell."

Shelley blinks, gasps for air.

"Honey, I *promise* you it's gonna turn out okay."

Shelley presses her eyes with her fingers. "I want, I just want, for her to be . . . for . . . *Elizabeth*."

R<small>AWLS'S</small> <small>STUDY</small>. Andrewjewski and Rawls. They're alone.

"But there are still two crucial points I've gotta repeat to you, Jim. I really must emphasize both of them."

"Go ahead."

"I know I've been through this already, but it's absolutely critical that Exley, the newspapers, that nobody gets wind of this insurance policy. The existence of this policy—"

"There's no way that's a problem, Burke. Really."

"An insurance company can't even be mentioned, they don't even mention it themselves in . . . It's for much the same reason, I guess, that you're not showing Exley that—"

"Either way, as I say, it's not the kind of thing that's a problem."

"Because the thing of it is, it's still rather iffy as to whether I *or* NorthCentral are actually covered on this. The policy explicitly states 'executive and members of his immediate family,' *whatever* they say in that letter."

"We're in a very gray area here. I can see that."

Rawls leans back on the couch, sips his coffee. "And there's no way in hell they'll decide on their liability in time to do *us* any good. So it's *my* ass that's gonna be out on the line."

"The people at Justice are even having a problem."

They are silent.

"And this isn't even to mention the long-range kinds of bullshit this causes. I mean, according to the way you've got me proceeding here, just about anybody can walk up and kidnap anyone else and start pressing these kinds of demands on some third party. Somebody's gotta draw the line *somewhere*."

"As soon as we get this Exley girl back we'll nip this thing in the bud."

"Nobody would be able to write these kinds of policies anymore."

They are silent.

"Is that bad, do you think?"

"I don't even know anymore. I've never liked the God-damn things to begin with. Although yes. I think that it might be."

"I don't know either."

They are silent.

"The point's that I'm turning out to be a pretty soft touch for these people, and we're not even certain the girl's—"

"Not really. Though I do see your point. But they haven't got away with it yet. Not by a long shot."

"No they haven't. They haven't. And yet, and no offense to you or your people, but right now I wouldn't bet a whole lot against them."

Andrewjewski takes a sip of his coffee. "And I take it, then, that the line you just mentioned should perhaps be drawn elsewhere. That Exley's daughter's—"

"No, I don't. Though I wish, I almost wish that I did feel that way, but I don't."

"The difference is . . . We've got to get that girl out in one piece. That's got to be the number-one thing. Once we do that we can really pull out all the stops and just—"

"Send in the linebackers."

"Linebackers, cornerbacks. Everyone."

They are silent.

"And we feel, and I certainly feel, that you've made the correct decision. And a very courageous and generous one."

They are silent.

"That's my business, I guess. Making right calls."

They touch cups.

"To exchange and recover then."

They raise up their cups.

"To the safeties."

On the channel 2 news, Walter Jacobson is describing Burke Rawls's background. A black-and-white photo of Rawls, fairly recent, has been superimposed onto the picture.

Albers and Brett, Herbert Dundee, and the Rawlses are seated around the glass-topped kitchen table, all of them watching the television. A cassette deck is running, and Albers takes notes on a pad.

"The Republican party's nominee for the Senate," says Jacobson, "only three years ago, he is currently chief executive officer and principal shareholder of NorthCentral Industries. He also serves on the boards of the Nuclear Regulatory Commission and the Illinois Arts Council. His wife, Anne Jaffe Rawls, of the Philadelphia Jaffes . . ."

No one in the kitchen says anything. Dundee clears his throat.

The station now cuts to John Drummond, who has positioned himself at the end of the Rawlses' long driveway.

Dundee shakes his head. "Jesus Christ."

Anne Rawls slowly stands up, takes her drink, and moves out into the living room.

The station's next shot is of the Exley's apartment upstairs from Killian's. A Hubbard Woods squad car is shown parked in the driveway. The reporter, Camilla Carr, points out that no lights are on at the Exleys'.

"Isn't Jack Exley there?" says Dundee. He looks over at Brett.

"He's down with his wife now," says Albers. "We took him down to the hospital. Otherwise he's staying with us."

Rawls lights a cigarette.

Carr throws it back over to Jacobson: "As we reported on our six-o'clock show, the Hubbard Woods hostage situation began around ten-thirty this morning, just as the children were out on the playground. But then"—he cocks his head slightly now, leaning forward—"it took a bizarre—"

"How could they have connected all this up with us already?" says Rawls. "This soon, I mean."

Anne Rawls returns to the kitchen.

"Actually," says Brett, "the big surprise is that they didn't manage to put two and two together by six."

"Do you think," says Anne. "Is Shelley Exley watching all this, do you think?"

Dundee says, "I hope not."

A Smith Barney commercial comes on.

"I don't think so," says Brett. "Most likely not."

"They must have her isolated, or tried to—"

"I hope not."

Rawls picks up the remote-control unit and switches to Channel 5: a commercial for Federal Express in which a bald young executive speaks very quickly.

No one smiles.

On Channel 7, Tim Weigl is reading a description of Exley: "... a lecturer in English at the University of Illinois at Chicago, the family has lived at the Hubbard Woods address for four years. Mrs. Exley is believed to be pregnant with—"

"Christ."

Anne Rawls strikes a match now and a particle of sulfur flies up into her eye. She winces and squints and cries out.

"You all right, honey?"

She shakes out the match. "Goddamnit, goddamnit, goddamnit."

"What happened?" says Albers. "What happened?"

"Or his balls just happened to go on sabbatical."

"Probably just doesn't feel like playing, you know, Agamemnon. I mean, especially with some other guy's daughter."

"Who knows."

"Sense of noblesse oblige just must've got to him."

"Who knows."

Six desk-top phones, all gray push-button models, are lined up about four inches apart from one another in a neat row across Rawls's desk. Each has a light blue label attached to its base. The label of the first phone on the left says "Downtown—Shields," and the one after that says "D.C." The next two labels say "Rawls," and the fifth one is blank. The sixth phone's label says "Exley."

Andrewjewski sits in a chair to the left of the desk, writing on a small yellow tablet. He stops writing a moment and stares at the phones, zeroing in on the one that says "Exley." He puts down his pen, stretches, stands up.

The six gray phones in a row, their surfaces reflecting the light of the fluorescent desk lamp, none of them ringing.

Andrewjewski continues to stretch.

THE CAR CARRYING EXLEY back from the hospital eases its way through a cluster of gawkers, reporters, and cameramen before it can finally turn into the driveway. Through the glare of the lights on the windshield the reporters appear almost frantic.

The car moves up the long driveway, bears right as it circles in front of the house, stops a few feet from the porch.

Exley gets out. Andrewjewski and Rawls are already out on the porch. The breath of all three is now visible.

"Anything?"

"Because even *one* million in cash, in, say, ten-dollar bills, is gonna weigh a lot more than you do. You multiply that—"

"Exactly. Same thing with gold."

"So either way you look at it—"

"Has to be diamonds. Just has to."

"Both'd still require current assets, however."

"You mean, what? Fluid?"

"Or liquid."

"You got it."

"Exactly. And what we're talking here is one fucking hellacious amount of liquidity."

B~URKE RAWLS STANDS~ by the door of his study. Andrewjewski gets up off the couch and takes off his suit jacket. Exley just sits there and smokes.

"I'll be back," says Rawls. "I just need some air. You two guys want something?"

Andrewjewski and Exley decline.

"I'll be back, then," says Rawls.

He goes out.

Exley gets up, stretches his legs and his back, coughs, sits down again on the couch. Andrewjewski loosens his tie.

They stare at each other.

"That's interesting."

"It is," says Andrewjewski. He brushes his black and gray stubble with the back of his hand. "In any event, there've been a number of other developments I'd like to go over with you. We just want to keep you apprised."

Exley nods.

"First of all, how is Shelley? We heard that—"

"So far she's stable. She's expecting—"

"That's good, Jack. That's what we all—"

"But she was definitely relieved to hear about Mr. Rawls's willingness to cooperate."

"Of course. So was I. And we've got two good men

down there at the hospital who'll be in constant contact up here."

"That's what they told me."

"Whenever you want to go down there again, visit her, just let me know."

"So what about these other developments."

"Okay. The first thing we want you to know, Jack, is that Mrs. Zigulski has died. She—"

"Jesus."

"Right."

Exley is silent.

"Apparently there was simply too much hemorrhaging, internal hemorrhaging, you know, for them to have saved her. But Russell Sigbe is fine."

"So how . . . I mean, good. That's good about Russell. Jesus. I'm real glad to hear, so but how does that—"

"We're going to try to keep Mrs. Zigulski's condition among ourselves for a while, Mr. Zigulski being the . . . At least till tomorrow at five. Because once these people—"

"It's just that—"

"Once these people become aware of something like this, the ante gets upped immeasurably. I'm sure you can see . . ."

Exley nods.

"Your line, by the way, the phone in your apartment, has been rerouted so that it will ring right in here on the desk. It's that one right there, and it'll light up if anyone calls on your line."

"My mother know that?"

"Your mother knows all about it, Jack. And she wants me to tell you, you can get in touch with her anytime at her apartment. We dropped her back home as soon as we'd rerouted the phones."

Exley nods.

"And what we'd like you to do is stay put right here with us for the night."

"Fine. But have you found out anything else about where they might have Elizabeth?"

"We've got five or six leads that we're working on, Jack. Even more than that, actually. We've got the car, for example, the—"

"You know, it's just that one of the problems I've got with all this . . . for example, about Mr. Zigulski . . ."

"Mrs. Zigulski. Right."

"Because if you're going, for practical purposes, going to keep something like that from Mr. Zigulski, and I certainly can understand—"

"You can see, Jack . . ."

"I mean, I'm all for doing anything, including, I'm in favor of doing whatever has to be done, whatever it takes . . . but it still makes me nervous."

"There's nothing, Jack. I know what you're thinking."

"Whatever it is, Mr. Andrewjewski, whatever the fuck it is, I wanna know about it."

"And you're going to, Jack. You are going to."

"Bad news, everything."

"And what I'm saying just now, for example. The car. We've now got the car they used at the school, and—and we're working on that."

Exley just stares at him.

"We've also talked to some post office people, plus we're tracing the typewri— you know, the basic somatotypes of the three in the car are being run through the computer in Washington."

"Which could . . . what?"

"And so when you supplement this with about three dozen interviews, what the eyewitnesses themselves have to say."

"Which is what?"

"And so as these things begin to develop more fully, Jack, you'll be the first one to know. Try to keep in mind it's still early."

"But she's been gone *since this morning*."

"Jack, I know that. Believe me I know it. But we're getting closer all the time. You've just got to trust me. The banks, for instance, the diamond brokers, they don't even open for business until eight or nine in the morning, our time, tomorrow."

They are silent. Exley crushes out what's left of a cigarette, begins to light up another one, stops. Andrewjewski takes a sip of his tea.

"Who the fuck *are* these fucking people?" says Exley. "I mean, when they called, do they say why they singled out Rawls?"

"That's another thing that we're working on. But just let me make one more point now, okay? You and I sit here. You see me, one single guy, but I'm by no means the whole operation. Right now there are hundreds of other leads getting followed up on by other people. There are things going on now downtown, back in Washington. The point, Jack, is that what you can't see while you're sitting here is that there's still a heck of a lot of pertinent stuff going down."

"I know that. So what?"

"We're pursuing this case very forcefully. It's just that it's hard for one person to appreciate more than a small percentage of it, no matter *how* involved he might be."

Exley nods.

"And what we're trying to do, Jack, is we're going to bring your daughter back home safe and sound."

They are silent.

"Anyway, to answer your question, our thinking as to

why they may have singled out Rawls. We're still working on this, but in the end it will probably have a lot to do with what we call his being a representative member of a certain social position. It's—"

"I've heard this already, though. Twice. Tells me *nada*."

"Our job's, though, not to . . . What I mean is, our thinking's been that, I expect the pieces to start coming together real soon."

They are silent.

"Tonight, do you think?"

"It's possible, Jack. Anything's possible."

Exley strikes a match now, stares at the flame for a while, lights a cigarette.

"Our success rate in cases like this, in domestic kidnapping cases of this sort we've had over a ninety-six percent rate of success."

Exley just exhales.

"Ninety-six percent, Jack. And we've got some sleeping pills out in the van by the way, Dalmanes I think, very safe, if you want to go up and lie down."

Exley says nothing.

"Might really do you some good, you know, help get you through all day tomorrow. There's not anything left you can do for a while."

"I'll pass," Exley says. "Not tonight."

"Although there's really not much else—"

"Not tonight."

1:45 TUESDAY MORNING.

Two slender girls, fifteen or sixteen, approach a small blue mailbox in west Hubbard Woods. Both are wearing track shoes, corduroy Levi's, and sweatshirts—one from Kalamazoo College, one from Northwestern. Far off-key, they are singing:

> *It's raining*
> *It's pouring*
> *The old man*
> *Is snoring . . .*

Just as they're passing the mailbox, at the last possible instant, the girl in the Northwestern sweat shirt pulls a small white card from her pocket and pushes it into the slot. Still singing—screaming now even, and laughing—the girls start to run. It is neither raining nor threatening to.

A white Chevrolet with M plates swerves into a driveway now and brakes hard in front of them, cutting them off. Two Cook County sheriffs jump out. A third man—bald, short, very muscular, wearing a dark tight turtleneck sweater—runs up behind them; a pair of binoculars hangs from his neck, and he is carrying a small two-way radio.

They speak to each other. The man in the turtleneck shows his identification. The girls have stopped laughing.

The Chevrolet's radio crackles and snaps as all five walk back toward the mailbox. The sheriffs' revolvers remain in their holsters.

The man in the turtleneck unlocks the mailbox, takes out the card—all that's inside—and starts reading. One of the sheriffs explains to the girls what has happened.

The man in the turtleneck looks up at one of the sheriffs, raises his eyebrows, then glances back down at the card. "Love notes on postcards these days?" he says, wincing and smiling.

The girls remain silent.

The man relocks the mailbox and slides the card back in the slot. "Please do excuse us," he says.

On Rawls's front lawn, near a tree, hidden from both the people inside the house and the reporters out front on the sidewalk, Exley stands by himself in the dark.

He pulls his hands from his pockets and looks at the sky through the branches. He pushes his hair off his forehead, shivers, scratches the back of his neck.

He remains standing in one position—head slightly lowered, forearms crossed on his chest, most of his weight on one foot—for more than a minute; he finally looks up to watch as one of the reporters and her minicam crew are restrained by a pair of policemen near the end of the driveway.

Somebody shouts.

A dog starts to bark.

Exley sits down on the grass but stands back up right away.

"A shout in the street," he says, to himself.

ANDREWJEWSKI, in Rawls's study, and Special Agent Vance Shields, in the Dirksen Building in downtown Chicago:

"We also interviewed the girls—"

"The cheerleaders?"

"Right. Although they were never really under all that much—"

"And so what were they doing then driving around, and in those uniforms too, ten o'clock on a school morning?"

"There was a picture-taking session scheduled at school. For the yearbook or something."

"And good reasons for arriving that late for their classes?"

"Afraid so."

"What about those other two, then, the ones had the accident?"

"Okay. The guy, Daryl Solomon—"

"Really beautiful timing, that goddamn thing."

"Couldn't have been worse, I don't think."

"Christ."

"Anyway, the man, Daryl Solomon, he checks out all the way. Three little kids, not all that—"

"Any college?"

"None. That's the thing. On his way downtown to his job, right on time, plus probably too old by half, kind of squirrelly—"

"Right."

"Either way, all his tees cross."

"So it's the woman, then . . ."

"Yeah."

"The girl in the other car."

"Right."

"What's the problem?"

"Two things so far. Nothing big."

"Any past?"

"None. Problem's that her roommate used to work for Burke Rawls's company."

"Hm."

"Right. As a secretary."

"Hm. For NorthCentral."

"Afraid so."

"Along with about seventeen thousand other people, though, I imagine."

"Right. Although never any contact with Rawls."

"Yeah, but still."

"Hm."

"Anyway, the roommate's name's Amy Slazinger. The driver was this Amy Cummings."

"Amy Amy."

"You got it. The thing of it is, Amy Cummings, the roommate, was a philosophy major at Madison. The driver, I mean."

"University of Wisconsin, you mean?"

"Yes. Amy Slazinger worked at NorthCentral seven, eight months back in, that's the roommate now, back in—"

"But she's willing to talk to us."

"Matter of fact, they've both been extremely cooperative."

They are silent.

"Okay then, Vance."

"Yeah."

"Let me know, especially about the items, those two little doodads you found in the Quantum."

"Don't worry."

"And nothing on Exley yet, right? Besides that poster thing Bancroft found in his office?"

"Not that I've heard of."

"All right then."

"Okay."

"Didn't really think so, I guess."

"Okay. Say hi to Janie."

"Will do. And let me know if your guys turn up anything else."

"Okay."

"Talk to you."

EXLEY AND BRETT at the glass-topped kitchen table, drinking coffee and smoking, alone.

Brett holds a stack of blue three-by-five cards and is tapping it square on the table. "Couple of other things, Jack, that we'd still like to know about. You still feel like talking?"

Exley unzips the cellophane of a fresh pack of Marlboro Lights then carefully tears a square off the top of the tinfoil liner. "What can I tell you?"

"Was Elizabeth"—Brett picks up one of the cards—"is she taking any form of medication?"

Exley packs a cigarette against the nail of his thumb. "Only thing she takes is one of those children's vitamins. Ones, you know, they're shaped like the Flintstones?"

Brett writes on one of the cards. "My kids take those too."

Exley lights the cigarette, says nothing.

"How does she tend to react during stressful situations?"

"Usually pretty well, I would say. When she doesn't get her way . . ." Exley shrugs. "She just sulks. She gets mad. But I wouldn't say she was much of a crier."

Brett writes again on the card.

"About the worst thing she's been through was when her mother had the last miscarriage. She was three. She was a little confused about Shelley's having been gone for those days."

"Sure," says Brett. He nods and starts writing again.

"I guess that's about—"

"And you and Shelley have never been separated."

Exley considers. "Actually, now that you ask me, we haven't."

Brett looks up and smiles. "That's good," he says. "How are you liking your job?"

"I like my job fine. There are better teaching jobs around I suppose, ones that pay a bit more—"

"But basically you're satisfied. Basically."

Exley nods. "Although what sort of difference could something like how much I happen to—"

"All we do, Jack, we just try to get as much background information as we can. Not just from you, of course. I'm talking *everybody*. Because you really can't tell when some little tidbit, some trivial little detail . . ."

Exley nods.

"How's Shelley doing now, by the way?"

"I really can't say. I don't think she knows at this point which thing she's supposed to be worried about."

"It's a real insidious situation, Jack. You and Shelley both have all of our sympathies. I've got two little kids of my own."

Exley nods.

"I really do mean that, Jack."

Exley is silent. Brett goes through the cards again now, rearranging them, occasionally writing things down.

"Listen, Brett, Alex . . . I know you can't make any promises—"

"I can't, Jack. I'd like to, you know. I'd love to be able to tell you—"

"Say you could. What would you say were the chances, the chances of her getting out of this . . . you know, soon."

"Right now I'd say they were excellent, but there's no way to determine something like that real exactly. Do you know what I mean?"

Exley nods.

"We can look at past cases, come up with some nice probabilities. I'd say they were excellent, though."

"Around ninety-six percent?"

"Around that high. Sure."

"But that's the percentage of hostages cases resolved successfully, though, is it not?"

"Something like that. The point's that if, that when the Rawlses come up with the money—"

"They will, don't you think? I mean, they wouldn't—"

"I know one thing they're doing is working some deal in New York that might get them a very good price, and that that could make a very big difference."

"And they wouldn't try to get fakes?"

"Completely out of the question. That's out of the question entirely. That much I *can* say. It was never even seriously considered."

They are silent.

"I know what you're thinking, Jack."

"You do."

"But believe me, the very worst thing you could do now is go running off to the papers, no matter how legitimate—"

"And you're certain that that's what I'm thinking."

"And it's a perfectly natural response."

"How do you mean?"

"Two reasons. The deadline we're under's incredibly tight as it is. You figure with the built-in delays, all the lag time just making the basic transactions, so that any *additional* PR complication would just undermine the whole process."

Exley puts out his cigarette.

"Look at it this way," says Brett. "You get six dozen TV people, print reporters frantically mucking around here thinking Pulitzer Prize, somebody latches onto a rift between the two principal parties, with us getting caught in the middle."

"It's one of the few cards I've got left in my hand."

"What we need to get your daughter back is maximum internal control and an absolute minimum of outside distractions." Brett lights a cigarette. "Burke Rawls is the one person now you do *not* want to alienate. There's also no way of telling how our adversaries might react. About the last impression you want to be leaving them with's that they might not get paid."

Exley says nothing.

"You follow me?"

"Let me explain something to you. When something like this happens to one of your children—"

"You want to do something about it."

"You're goddamn fucking right you wanna do something about it."

"I know it. I know."

"Yeah. You know. So then tell me one thing. What if they get what they want and they *still* won't release her?"

"That's extremely unlikely. And it's not gonna happen. We also fully expect to have located them by then, have them—"

"Yeah yeah yeah. But what if you don't."
"That's one thing you don't have to worry about."
"So if by then—"
"Because we're definitely gonna have found them."
"Although by *then* . . ."

DOWNTOWN HUBBARD WOODS. Two lights are on, behind curtains, in the apartment above Chestnut Court Bookstore. A traffic light switches from yellow to red. The only other light comes from two streetlights, from the mauve haze of dawn to the east, and from the indirect industrial panels through the translucent post office windows.

In the crowded, chaotic sorting room forty-four clerks, subs, and carriers are yawning, yodeling, smoking, working their cases, drinking coffee from thermoses, complaining out loud to one another. Five three-tiered gurneys of first-class mail stacked in gray plastic trays are wheeled in off one of the docks. A young white mail carrier is whanging air-guitar bar chords. Another one sings "Start Me Up."

Carrier E. Norman Smith is quietly tossing cards, small parcels, and letters into the various slots of case 26. Each item for 1900 Sheridan Road, however, Smith hands to the tall red-haired SOAR agent standing beside him. The agent immediately slits open these envelopes with the blade of a Swiss army knife, briefly examines the contents, then slides both contents and envelope into a cream-colored folder.

Two aisles away, at case 42, Lewis Mason is putting aside all mail addressed to the Exleys. It now sits in a small pile just to the left of the case: two third-class fliers from stores in the Loop, a postcard from Shelley's dentist reminding her that she is due for a checkup, a BankAmericard statement, a first-class letter from Tucson.

The agent in charge of intercepting the Exleys' mail—he is black, young, with round gold-framed glasses—is up front at the special-delivery table, thumbing through the thick stack of packages, manila envelopes, and letters.

He stops now, breathes in and looks up at the clock, then pulls out a plain white business-size envelope addressed to "Burke Rawls, Esquire."

He sniffs, clears his throat, and stands up.

"Because you can fudge a small bit on the color, save yourself, you know . . . even use VVS$_2$'s."

"Difference between a D and an F in a three-carat would still be forty, fifty percent."

"Forty thousand each as opposed to twenty-four."

"You think Rawls would go for it?"

"The question is, would those people out there be able to tell the difference?"

"Right. But the *real* question is—"

"Did they specify brilliant and round, do you know?"

"I don't know. Though the big question's, how—"

"Call him back up and find out."

"You call him, then."

"Just call him. It's the only way we're gonna find out."

"Or call what's his name . . . Andrewjewski."

"Better call Rawls. Call Rawls first. *Then* you call Andrewjewski."

"No return address?" says Rawls.

"None," says Andrewjewski, "P.M. Loop postmark. Good morning."

"Good morning."

"There've already been six or eight sets of prints smudged together all over the envelope."

"Mm."

"Doubt very much there'll be any inside."

Rawls sips his coffee.

"Better try this on," says Andrewjewski. He hands Rawls a white latex glove; he already wears one himself. "Just in case. We'll try to touch the upper right corner only."

Rawls puts down his coffee, pulls on the glove. "I knew *some*body'd have to bend over eventually."

Andrewjewski slits open the envelope, looks up at Rawls, then pulls out a single sheet of heavy white bond; folded twice, it is identical to the sheet on which the ransom letter was typed. Rawls watches Andrewjewski's face as he opens it up and starts reading.

At the center of the sheet the outline of a small child's right hand has been traced in soft lead. A fingernail clipping has been glued to the top of the middle finger at the spot where the real nail would end; a neat dotted line has been drawn through a point two thirds of the way down the same finger. A second dotted line cuts across where the wrist would be. Two inches under the hand, printed in navy-blue ink in block letters, a note: FINGER'S NEXT, BURKE OLD BOY, AND WE'RE SURE IT'S YOUR FAVORITE. AFTER THAT WE'RE LOOKING AT THE PROVERBIAL INVISIBLE HAND. DO DELIVER.

Andrewjewski hands Rawls the sheet; their gloved thumbnails touch as the sheet changes hands. "All they're doing with this is stepping up their asthenic game plan. Nothing more."

Rawls examines the drawing, the note.

"What I mean, what I mean is that nothing has changed."

"I can see that."

Andrewjewski says nothing.

"They'd go this far?" Rawls doesn't look up. "Do you think?"

"A communication like this is more or less what we expected."

"Christ . . ."

"What it is, the point is that *their* point was already made Monday morning. This communication here, it's merely redundant."

Rawls continues to stare at the drawing.

"Do you know what I mean?"

"I can see what it is," says Rawls. He looks up. "And I can see what it says."

Andrewjewski attempts, gently, to take back the sheet, and for a second or two Rawls won't let go.

ANNE RAWLS, in a navy-blue terrycloth robe, comes out of the bathroom drying her hair with a towel, and humming.

Rawls stands on the other side of the room by the bureau, trying—unable—to read the *Tribune*.

"Shower's all yours now."

Rawls only nods.

"Sheila and Ellen both called, wanted to book a flight home. I told them you told me that you wanted them to wait for a while."

Rawls puts down the paper. "I talked to them too. I mean, it's better if they stay where they are. They just got settled there, what? Four or five days ago?"

"That's what I told them."

Thirty-five seconds of silence. Anne sits down on the bed.

"Those two poor poor people."

"Yeah," says Rawls. He picks up one of the two cups of coffee on top of the bureau and carries it over to Anne.

"I think I'll try to stick with coffee today," says Anne. "Or maybe some wine."

"Please do."

"I'm going to try."

They are silent.

"I'd like to think," says Rawls. He stares at the lake. "I'd like to be able to think we're no worse off now having things . . . only *now,* there's no way we're just as upset as I'd be if they *had* taken Veevee."

Anne sips her coffee; they look at each other.

"Because, though I realize it couldn't possibly be the same thing."

"We were just lucky I guess."

Rawls sits down on the bed. "It's just that we have to admit, not having known ahead of time how things would turn out . . . it's almost as though"—he gets up and goes to the window—"we're almost, not *happy,* just that I much prefer them not to have *her.*"

"Jeez, of course . . ."

"But it's not all that simple, not for us. I mean insurance, no insurance . . ." He switches on the "Today Show."

"For them *or* for us."

Willard Scott is discussing "national live color radar." Rawls turns down the sound. Turns it off.

"You going running this morning?"

"Ah, no. I don't think I'm going running this morning."

Another long silence.

"This Andrewjewski fellow seems to be a pretty good man."

"He does," says Rawls. "I suppose that he probably is."

"And, and so you think that he's got the Rx?"

They look at each other; both take sips of their coffee.

"I think he just might."

"Unless of course they can find—"

"The job he's got now's a damn tough one."

Bryant Gumbel comes on. The "Today Show" continues in silence.

"And so there's a chance that we'd, you know, get . . . ?"

"I really don't know. He says so, talks percentages, all their tactics and strategies, but I really don't know."

"What about the insurance, though?"

They are silent. Jane Pauley comes on.

"Just don't know . . . I mean I'm not sure about *that* business either."

They are silent.

"Mm."

The "Today Show" continues in silence.

In the doorway to the Rawlses' living room, on Exley's way in, Albers hands Exley an envelope. "Telegram," he says. "They delivered it to your apartment this morning."

Exley takes it and thanks him.

"I'm sorry we had to open it, but . . . Sorry."

Exley reads:

MR AND MRS JOHN EXLEY   DEPARTMENT OF ENGLISH
2933½ GREEN BAY ROAD   UNIVERSITY OF ILLINOIS
HUBBARD WOODS IL 60093   AT CHGO
                         BOX 4348
                         CHICAGO IL 60680

AND ALL SHALL BE WELL AND

ALL MANNER OF THING SHALL BE WELL

                      YOUR COLLEAGUES AND FRIENDS

Exley crumples the sheet, pauses, looks at the fireplace, then slowly uncrumples it.

He reads it again.

He folds it three times, presses out some of the wrinkles.

He slides it down into his pocket.

"I'VE GOT THE insurance people downtown looking at the damn thing right now," says Rawls. "Sandy too. We've also been in touch all last night with the guy in New York."

Andrewjewski nods and sits down.

Listening, waiting, Rawls holds one of the phones to his ear. "They've got me on hold at my own goddamn company."

Andrewjewski smiles, shakes his head.

"Main guy's not there yet," says Rawls. Into the phone: "And you called him at home? Right . . . all right . . . yes."

"The problem—"

"The problem's, I know. The problem is that if we don't decide one way or the other by, when? ten New York time, then as far as the deadline's concerned—"

"Your decision may as well have been no."

"All I can say is," says Rawls. Into the phone: "All right, Linda . . . right . . . yes. Soon as he walks in the door." He hangs up. "Sandy Lennon's already been through the damn thing."

"And?"

"And that clause, one about 'members of the immediate

family,' she says she expects them to play that one pretty cagey."

"They might, they might not choose to see it as North-Central's problem."

"You got it."

"Although—"

"Or theirs."

"Right. Although listen, Burke. Even if they don't assume liability right off the bat, and this isn't really my province, or, or exactly our jurisdiction, but would you and Anne still be able—"

"Yes and no."

They are silent.

"What you're saying's then, maybe some part of it?"

"Depends, all depends on the price we get from—"

"Or possibly just during some interim, some sort of escrow account?"

"What I mean is, all along we've been shelling out these incredible premiums . . . that they'll see their way clear to pay off."

Andrewjewski just nods.

"But so, I don't know."

"And yet as far as your own personal resources are concerned, that in other words—"

"In other words, maybe."

"You don't know."

"I don't know."

They are silent.

"We think," says Rawls. "Therefore we have to assume—"

"When could you know, though? By when can you know?"

"That if I *did* have to use my own resources, that somehow in the end they'd get recovered."

"Of course."

They are silent.

"Because I know that last night I promised you—"

Andrewjewski just holds up his hand. "Burke, I realize you have to make your decision as the information comes in to you."

"I mean, we'd be busted."

"Unless we recovered them."

"Unless you recovered them."

They are silent.

"That's routine procedure, Burke. That's routine standard procedure."

The sky over Lake Michigan is bright, light blue, and cool—it looks almost white—as the high-pressure system continues over the area. A contrail fades out to the south.

Stuart Juce, Killian's refrigerator and appliance repairman, is turned away by three Cook County sheriffs at the foot of the Rawlses' driveway; he had had an appointment at ten, but the Rawlses just now have canceled. Reporters converge on his dark orange van, shooting pictures and video tape, maneuvering, shouting questions in through the window. Juce just waves and drives off.

Cutting back across Sheridan Road, a middle-aged female reporter is nearly run down by a Mazda. She curses and takes off her sunglasses.

One of the reporters makes a joke about "available light," "one's own young ass," and "our own Mrs. Pettibone."

Jewel's delivery jeep, carrying cheese, Coke, bread, Wheaties, mayonnaise, mustard, peanut butter, cigarettes, apples, pears, two bags of ice cubes, cantaloupe, strawberry preserves, English muffins, sixteen TV dinners, paper towels, napkins, and ham for the Rawlses is allowed to pass through.

"To get a window shade, you know, to catch where you want it," says one of the photographers, "you can pull it down only so hard."

The Rawls house, the sun just above it, its shadow across the circular end of the driveway, as the Jewel jeep pulls up by the porch.

Two minicam operators, leaning against one of their vans, break open a six-pack of root beer.

"Days like this . . ."

"On days like this, what?"

They both take sips of their root beer.

A̲ndrewjewski hands Exley the phone that's marked "Exley"; it's just rung a fifth time.
"Hello."
Young male voice, cracking: "John P. Exley?"
"This is he."
Andrewjewski, listening in on the headphones, gestures to indicate that the conversation should continue.
"John Exley whose kid's just been kidnapped?"
"That's correct. Could you—"
"Well, do the Lindy, man." Background noise. Laughter. "Do the Lindy."
"Could you say . . ."
The young man hangs up then.

MICHAEL TIARNAHAN slides his brown leather briefcase onto the conveyor belt at the security checkpoint for O'Hare's Concourse C. He is wearing a charcoal wool suit, a blue Oxford shirt, a purple and navy silk tie. He takes out his keys and drops them into the square plastic tray that the Guardsmark guard holds out in front of him. He seems somewhat nervous. He gets into line, waits fifteen seconds, looks at his watch, then steps through the rectangular arch of the scanner.

At the other end of the conveyor belt, beyond the magnometer, two guards stand over his briefcase along with an elderly Chicago police sergeant. Open now, his briefcase contains two manila envelopes, sunglasses, reading glasses, some folders, an apple, a black leather pouch with a drawstring, *Dubliners,* a folded *Tribune* turned to the page with Elizabeth Exley's school picture, and handcuffs.

Tiarnahan pulls out his wallet. "I can explain those," he says. He looks at the sergeant and smiles. "I completely forgot all about them."

ANDREWJEWSKI stands in front of the blackboard, upon which he has already written five phrases. He is wearing a blue shirt now instead of a white one, a maroon tie instead of a blue one. He has showered and shaved, and he doesn't look tired.

"All the evidence so far," he says. "The evidence is that she still is alive. The Polaroid, the note itself, this message this morning. We shall therefore proceed on that basis."

Albers and a new agent, Mark Knopfler, are seated on the small leather couch. Beside them, in chairs, are two Hubbard Woods police lieutenants and a man from the Cook County Sheriff's Office. Two junior agents are standing.

"Though in all candor," says Andrewjewski, "we're not all that far off the ground yet. We haven't washed out any theories so far—"

"I assume you're not ready to talk to the press yet."

"Not by a long shot."

"No way."

"We've got the getaway car," says Albers. "We have a typescript from a ten-pitch IBM Correcting Selectric typewriter. We have what's left of those two slugs from the woman's Skorpion pistol."

"So it *was* a woman, then."

"By all accounts," says Knopfler. "Mrs. Witt, even a few of the kindergartners..."

"So that's what we're gonna assume."

"We've interviewed almost two hundred people along the likeliest escape routes. The consensus seems to be that first they went north, along those two side streets, toward Glencoe—"

"Yeah, we've been getting 'hot tips' on that all day long."

"Right."

"But when the Quantum finally turned up it was in Evanston, over by the Orrington Hotel."

"Which is eight or ten miles from any Glencoe."

"And in the goddamn opposite direction."

"And so we're working on that."

"Secondly, we have no reason at all to infer they'll extend this deadline, or be willing to negotiate on the diamonds, or even on the procedure for making the exchange. It's therefore imperative that we begin to make some sort of headway in our efforts to locate them."

"Our adversaries, as a group, appear to be a combination of vaguely leftish, vaguely political young men and women, college educated—"

"Unemployed..."

There is laughter.

"And from looking at these analogies, the prose, most likely majoring in something to do with the humanities."

"English, philosophy..."

"We'll be looking at this later more closely."

"And at the same time just good old-fashioned extortionists."

"We estimate their number to be between three and, three being the absolute minimum, and our best guess is it's probably closer to eight, maybe ten."

"We also estimate that the network of roadblocks set up, the helicopter surveillance, turned out to be an effective one. We think that it was."

"We think so too."

"Which leaves us with the reasonable possibility that the safe house is close to, even inside, Hubbard Woods."

"A door-to-door's being orchestrated right now by Chief Finn. He's the one you—"

"One question."

"In a second," says Andrewjewski. "I want to get through this business first and get you guys started before—"

"Fine."

"One of the most difficult aspects is that, at least if we go by the language, the note's implications just won't let us infer that the principles governing an exchange would be commutative."

"Ahm . . ."

The men stare down at their Xeroxes.

"In other words, they never come out or never explicitly state that if we turn over the diamonds the girl would be freed."

"We're bringing a linguist up here, guy from the U. of C., someone to take a good look at this stuff."

"But even if they came out and said she'd come back, we still wouldn't have a whole lot of reason to trust them."

"True. Our experience, however, is that if at some point they put it in writing, or say it out loud, they tend in the end to come through."

"That's interesting."

"Yeah. I'd heard that somewhere."

"Although it *is* just a tendency."

"What we can be certain about is that they'll act at each

stage in their own best interests, whatever they might perceive them to be."

"In other words—"

"Unless we can find them."

"Even if we don't, and he does pay, where's their incentive to reciprocate? Their deep-rooted charitable impulses?"

"Please don't interrupt me," says Andrewjewski. "It continues to appear that we have no real choice but, besides stepping up our efforts to locate them, but to gather together this money."

"Okay."

"The next thing," he says. He turns then and points to the blackboard. "This we can probably skip now. But this *next* thing . . ."

Tiarnahan on the phone in an unenclosed booth across the concourse from gate C-16. "I'm here," he says. "Right."

He stares across the concourse at the passengers' waiting area, listening to the person on the other end of the phone, sliding his boarding pass in and out of his pocket. The passengers have begun to line up to board.

"Right," he says. "Right . .,. I know that . . . of course. So it's settled then . . . all but for . . . right."

He hears music and turns. Two young men in black leather jackets go by, carrying guitar cases, magazines, binoculars, flowers. One of them is smoking a long thin cigar; the other has a portable cassette deck slung over his shoulder with the volume turned low. The live version of "Watching the Detectives" is playing.

"Twelve-twenty-something," says Tiarnahan. He watches the two men disappear in the crowd down the concourse. "Sure . . . one, about one—" He takes the boarding pass all the way out of his pocket, opens his ticket, and reads it. "Right . . . right. And get, get back the hour on the flight back in here."

He looks at his watch, listens; stares at the ceiling.

"Got it," he says. He puts the pass back in his pocket.

"And he'll meet me back here then? . . . Okay. At . . . at . . . right. So . . . so, right . . . so I'll see you."

He hangs up the phone, crosses the concourse, then goes back to pick up his briefcase.

In line by the gate he looks at his watch again—not really seeing what time it is—then turns his left hand, makes half a fist, and begins to examine his fingernails.

The line begins to move forward.

RAY SIGBE CARRIES RUSSELL down the second-floor hall of the hospital. Russell's head rests on his father's left shoulder, but he jerks it up suddenly now, giggling. He has just been released. Marilyn Sigbe reaches up and runs her right hand through his hair.

The Sigbes emerge from an elevator, make two left turns down a corridor, and arrive at the nurses' station outside of Shelley's room. Ray Sigbe sits down with Russell; Marilyn speaks to one of the nurses. The nurse points her across the hall to the blue-suited agent who is sitting outside room 3133 reading *Sports Illustrated.*

The agent and Mrs. Sigbe stand outside Shelley's door. The IV unit is still hooked up to her arm and the sideguards of the bed have been raised. Shelley is sleeping. There are flowers and cards on the windowsill.

The Sigbes stand by the elevator. The agent presses the down button and waits with them there till the down light goes off. Mrs. Sigbe hands the agent a small slip of paper. He takes it, smiles, says "We will," and puts it into his pocket. He shakes Ray Sigbe's hand.

Russell giggles.

"Noonbreak," in progress, on Channel 2 News.

LEE PHILLIP: And we've been probing today this question with Mrs. Glenna Saint John, a psychic, or medium, from Akron, Ohio. Our number again is 555-6340.

The picture shows Mrs. St. John, wearing a dark green plaid suit, with the phone number superimposed just below her. A man's arm and hand and the side of a chair appear on the edge of the screen to her left.

MRS. ST. JOHN: All I'd like to do is try to help bring this nightmare to an end. As I said, I don't want to say, and I can't say now who, where, things like when . . .

LEE PHILLIP: But you've seen, you say you have *seen* where Elizabeth Exley is now being held.

MRS. ST. JOHN: Yes, I have.

LEE PHILLIP: Although could you say again just what you mean when you say you have *seen* her?

MRS. ST. JOHN: Doctors have told me, very reputable doctors, that in every molecule in the world, there is activity, which sends out, you know, *more* activity. Some people are more receptive to this than others. The scientists seem to think that it has something to do with the fluid that coats all our nerves. Some people just have more of it than others.

LEE PHILLIP: And so in this way, via these certain vibrations, you are able to—

MRS. ST. JOHN: I can see her, Miss Phillip, see her at times now, before me at times, in my mind.

LEE PHILLIP: And you can actually *see* Elizabeth Exley.

MRS. ST. JOHN: But I can't say at this time, and I would do nothing to hurt the police investigation. We've already—

LEE PHILLIP: And you're here in Chicago at their request and expense.

MRS. ST. JOHN: Yes.

LEE PHILLIP: And so, could you evaluate for us now, in terms of—

MRS. ST. JOHN: But I would never, and I have never charged a penny for the use of my gift.

555-6340 comes on the screen again.

Lee Phillip smiles at Mrs. St. John, then looks at the camera. "We'll be back," she says, "taking calls, as 'Noonbreak' continues."

"But the other thing about seven, let's see, the middle of seven, he seems to be playing with some sort of rhyme scheme."
"I noticed that too."
"How do you mean?"
"C.O.D.'s, guarantees."
"Reads like iambic pentameter."
"Mm."
"Come again?"
"Might be iambic, but it sure as hell isn't pentameter."
"It's close enough."
"Close enough for what? That's my whole point."
"Da*da* da*da* da*da* C.O.D.'s, right? Da*da* da*da* da*da* guarantees."
"There's twenty-four syllables—"
"There's at least two extra feet in there, though."
"And twenty-one in the second."
"No, twenty."
"And we're supposed to infer from all this that he's engaging, or she is, in what? In some sort of grisly poetics?"
"Because whether it scans—"
"But to what *conceivable* purpose—"

"Wait a second. Just wait a second. Where are you at now?"

"Ain't you ever heard of free verse?"

"Number seven."

"Right."

"Seven again?"

"Right. Give me Librium or give me meth."

"It's like the Shakespeare business in one."

"You mean like, like it's some sort of code?"

"Actually it's quite a different business in seven."

"My question is, what could *possibly* be the difference between whether it rhymes, how it rhymes, or it doesn't? Because as far as *we* are concerned—"

"Maybe they're playing it cute, tossing out some weird brand of cryptic horsewash or something."

"Although the point's that—"

"If there *is* any code—"

"And what's this business about the Illinois Arts Council? Rawls's already established he has no connection with that."

"Not even indirectly. We've had that checked out."

"The companies make steel, batteries, do some bottling. Nothing, you know, that could be even remotely construed—"

"The point, gentlemen, is that the author of this missive has clearly taken a great deal of care with the precise wording of each point he makes, and that, therefore, we would be well advised to examine it with the same sort of perspicacity they put into it."

"Perspicacity, huh."

"And find what?"

"I don't know yet. We can't know that till we look."

"I'll be back in a minute."

"This is obviously an intelligent, literate person we're

dealing with here. So it only makes sense that the exact words he chose should impact somehow on how we respond to them."

"I thought that decision's already been made."

"The note with the hand's an even better example."

"Or the typo in eight."

"Or the typo in eight."

"You done with that ashtray?"

"What typo in eight?"

"There's a typo in eight. Least there was. The *k* in kill was originally typed as a *b*."

"Although anyone can make a typing mistake, you expect the error, a regular error, to occur as the typist attempts to hit *k* on the keyboard; one expects the error to turn out either *j, i, o, l, m,* or comma. Some are more likely than others, depending on the subsequent letters, but in general one of the letters surrounding it is what you're expecting."

"But never a *b*?"

"A *b* just is not what you'd predict."

"This was one of those big new IBM jobs they were using, was it not?"

"Whereas the *c* in *insufficient* in four was originally typed as a *v*. Now *that* you'd expect."

"Bookface Academic seventy-two."

"You can't see this, of course, on your Xeroxes, but when you turn the original over you clearly make out which key he'd hit first."

"They're already out at IBM in Des Plaines trying to trace it."

"But that note with the fingernail, about the invisible hand?"

"Mind running that by us again?"

"The invisible hand is straight Adam Smith. Basically

it's what supposedly keeps a free market functioning, intact."

"To the point now, guys. Please."

"What our friend here is getting at is just one more of his sorry-ass plays on words, one more attempt to goad Rawls, who he apparently sees as some sort of—"

"As an insidious purveyor of systemic violence."

"Well he is, ain't he?"

"Not funny."

"That's not funny."

"Okay okay. It's not funny."

"To the point please, guys."

"It's not funny."

GENEVIEVE WAVES an old piece of lime-green hula hoop at Frances, her golden retriever. Frances arches her back and starts yipping. The sun casts their shadows almost straight down onto the grass of the Rawlses' backyard; most of the grass is still green.

Genevieve brushes the end of the hoop in the grass. A bright yellow sunfish slides by through the trees a hundred yards out on the lake.

Genevieve rears back and tosses, not very far, and Frances is on top of the hoop in a flash. Genevieve hollers "Fetch!"

Frances returns to Genevieve's feet but refuses to give up the hoop.

"Good girl," says Genevieve, reaching down. "Oh, you! I mean bad girl!"

She grabs for the hoop again, laughing, but Frances draws back.

After twenty-five seconds of this, Frances accidentally-on-purpose allows the hoop to be snatched from her teeth.

Burke Rawls looks on from a first-story window; it is difficult to make out his face because of the dazzle of foliage and sun on the glass. He just watches.

Genevieve tosses the hoop, much farther this time, and Frances mad-dashes after it.

Three stories up, on the roof, a tactical officer with binoculars leans against one of the gables, staring past Frances and Genevieve out toward the boat on the lake.

Wagging her tail, with the hoop in her mouth, Frances barks.

"People die."
"Yes they do."
"Although some just not soon enough."
"Gentlemen, gentlemen . . ."
"These rights, those rights, I mean, so we really can't be all that surprised when we end up with this kind of an aggressively mindless Pink Floyd hodgepodge of a rhetorical, you know, from the people you're dealing with here."
"Give that a rest now, okay?"
"Well, as official member of the aforementioned press-ocracy—"
"You end up assuming every white dude in a suit's out to screw you is what it comes down to."
"No pun intended."
"Old news, guys. What can I tell you?"
"Wrong. Wrong wrong wrong wrong wrong."
"The social and economic climate has made this inevitable."
"Exactly. All this manure about cost-effective and what it's—"
"It's just now coalescing, my friend. Just now beginning to coagulate."

"Too many swinging dicks out there diddling with the Monopoly money."
"You got it."
"Socioeconomic perversity in Chicagoland."
"You got it."

E<small>XLEY AND KNOPFLER</small>, Knopfler driving, head south on Sheridan Road in one of the FBI's gray Impalas.

They pass four or five joggers, a hitchhiker wearing a scrub shirt and blue jeans, a small panel truck pulled over by a Kenilworth squad car. Exley just stares straight ahead.

Knopfler hesitates before speaking, then finally says, "How's she doing?"

Exley doesn't respond for a moment. Then: "You mean my wife?"

"Yeah. She okay?"

"She's okay," Exley says. He looks out the window. "They seem to be taking good care of her."

"Well, that's good."

They are silent again.

They pass Plaza del Lago, a Wilmette road crew patching some potholes, two older women on bicycles. Knopfler looks at his watch.

They wait at a red light in silence. Knopfler rolls down his window. They move forward again.

They pass Bahai Temple. Its white, latticed convexity gleams in the sunlight. Knopfler stares.

"You play tennis?" says Exley.

"With my wife," Knopfler says. He's dismayed. "Not so hot, though. Just picked it up, oh, about a—"

"I played a point once," says Exley. He does not look at Knopfler.

"A point? You mean, a game?"

"Some guy I'd never played with before. I was filling in for somebody. Somebody must've got sick."

Knopfler tries to make eye contact and still drive the car. Exley stares forward.

"A very long point," Exley says, finally. "Ferocious practically. Deep ground strokes, lots of wide angles. Real crucial point in the set."

"You been playing awhile?"

"Guy finally takes a short ball I give him, slices it back to my forehand, comes in. The guy was left-handed, had all kinds of English . . . Anyway, I manage to get down to the ball and hook it back crosscourt, heavy topspin, almost a mishit in fact. The guy must've guessed down the line. Passed him cleanly."

"Sounds like a pretty good shot," says Knopfler. "Sounds like—"

Exley turns now and faces him. "He brings up his racquet then . . . I'm just standing there now, point's all over and all, and pretends like he's making the volley. He follows the ball with his eyes, completely ignoring, you know, completely ignoring the ball I'd hit past him, then watches this other imaginary ball up in the air and starts backing up, backpedaling, you know, as though *I'd* gone over, made a play on that volley that *he'd* made, and put up a lob of my own."

Exley keeps staring at Knopfler, but Knopfler has his eyes on the road now.

"He keeps right on backpedaling," says Exley, "keeping his head up, he's still following the arc of this lob I've supposedly hit, watches it bounce a couple of feet past his service line. Then he backs up some more, brings his racquet back over his shoulder, lets the ball bounce, cocks his wrist, then grunts and pretends like he's hitting this gargantuan overhead smash for a winner."

They turn into the driveway of Evanston Hospital. Knopfler is silent.

"Good get, the guy says," Exley says.

Knopfler is silent. He pulls up next to the entrance and stops.

Exley coughs violently. Again. And again. Very violently.

"So . . . so what did you say to the guy?"

Exley grimaces now, curling forward, crossing his forearms and hugging his chest and his rib cage.

"You okay?"

Exley coughs again, hard, grits his teeth. His face is all red.

Knopfler gets out of the car, runs around the front of it, opens up Exley's door.

"I've got to," says Exley. "Get my . . ."

Knopfler looks around, sees two attendants standing near the door of the hospital, signals and calls out for help.

A BRIGHTLY LIT SLIDE is projected onto a portable screen at the end of the almost dark study: Burke Rawls giving a speech. He is standing behind a black rostrum in a blue pinstripe suit on a stage draped with red, white, and blue linen bunting. His hair is darker and shorter, more slicked back, than it is at the moment, as he sits and stares up at the screen.

The slide advancer clicks forward, the screen darkens, another slide drops into place: a small blond girl in a green and blue bathing suit, squinting up into the sun.

"Elizabeth over the summer," says Andrewjewski.

Dust and smoke swirls through the bright shaft of light. Someone coughs. The projector continues to hum.

The next slide, black and white, shows Elizabeth in pigtails, her mouth open wide in a shout. She's sitting on Jack Exley's shoulders.

"The most recent shot we can get hold of," says Andrewjewski. "Besides the school picture. Taken about six, seven weeks ago."

The next slide shows Elizabeth staring wide-eyed into the camera. She's wearing her Cubs jacket. The background is dark and unfocused.

"The Polaroid that came with the letter," says Andrewjewski. "Lab boys downtown managed to come up with this slide."

Next: an extreme close-up, cropped and blurry, of the previous slide of Elizabeth.

"Pay attention now," says Andrewjewski. "This is Elizabeth..." The next slide shows another young girl, also blond, also with pigtails, sitting on top of a pony. "And this is Genevieve Rawls. It might not be all that easy to see the resemblance, but even from these angles..."

The next slide shows Elizabeth again, sitting between her parents this time. Both she and Shelley had blinked as the film was exposed. Exley is drinking a beer.

"So if we can imagine them both wearing braids, almost exactly the same weight and height..." Andrewjewski gets up now and turns on the overhead light. "They tended as well to wear these little Cubs jackets, these little baseball jackets, two, three times a week in this weather, according to both of their parents..."

The projector still hums as he talks. The image on the screen of the Exleys' three faces can be made out hardly at all anymore, in the light.

"Plus we happen to know that Elizabeth often would cut..."

EXLEY, HIS SHIRT OFF, his elbows raised over his shoulders, standing inside one of the curtained-off cubicles of the emergency room. Dr. Padma Radmasamgi stands just behind him. Reaching around his broad back, she's wrapping the middle part of his torso with elastic gauze tape.

"Fracture caused wholly by stress," says the doctor. She tears off the gauze with her fingers. "When you coughed it just happened."

Exley nods.

"I have seen this before," says the doctor. "When under great stress." She tapes down the end of the gauze. "There. Very good."

"I thought I was having a heart attack."

"No no no no," says the doctor. She laughs, shakes her head. "Pain is much different." She winces as though in great pain.

Gingerly, very slowly, Exley lowers his arms to his sides.

"Look," says the doctor. She leads Exley over and points to the backlit display panel where two X-ray negatives, front view and side, of Exley's chest are displayed. "And your EKG, Jack, that was okay."

Exley raises his arms, lowers them, turns his shoulders, testing the pull of the tape. He coughs, winces, coughs.

"Though much too much smoking," says the doctor. She points to a thin dark horizontal line on the lowest left rib. "You can see?"

Exley moves a step closer and looks. The doctor moves out of the way.

"Yeah," Exley says. "Yes. You can just make it out."

"It is clear."

Exley smiles, shakes his head. "My first broken bone."

"Will heal in six weeks. Maybe eight. Your heart is okay."

Exley nods.

"Okay then?"

"Okay."

"And make certain you fill the prescription," says the doctor. "And then take them."

"I will."

She helps him on with his shirt.

"Thanks a lot . . . Thank you. You'll have to excuse the state of this shirt. I mean, it must be sort of funky by now."

"I have seen this before," says the doctor.

GLENNA ST. JOHN, alone on the couch in Rawls's study, kneading and twisting one of Elizabeth's T-shirts.

The Rawlses, Brett, Albers, and two other agents look on.

After thirty seconds or so, Mrs. St. John appears to go into a trance. A tape deck is activated. Albers puts up his finger.

Mrs. St. John remains in the trance for more than a minute. The others are silent.

Mrs. St. John begins speaking, in what is apparently Elizabeth's voice. "Tomorrow," she says. Then she is silent; it's as though she has cut herself off.

"What," says Anne. "Tomorrow what?"

Albers gestures for her to be quiet, but Anne just ignores him. "What will happen tomorrow, Mrs. Saint John?"

"The house next to Audrey's," says Mrs. St. John. "The great big blue one." The voice is a childish whine now. "I'm here, Daddy," it says. "I really am here now."

Anne sits down beside her. "Elizabeth . . ."

Albers shushes the others.

Mrs. St. John remains silent.

"Mrs. Saint John," says Anne. "Is Elizabeth—"

"Anne."

Mrs. St. John closes her eyes, trembles, look up at Rawls. "Hmmm?"

"Is Elizabeth speaking now? Did you see her?"

"Jesus," says Rawls.

"Hmmm?" says Mrs. St. John. She seems more herself now. "Did you see her?"

"I think that we may have," says Albers. To Anne: "Who is Audrey?"

"One of their friends," says Anne. "One of their classmates. Audrey Boorstin, I think."

Albers nods at Brett, looks back at Anne. "B-O-O-R-S-T-I-N?"

"I think so."

"She live in Hubbard Woods?"

"Yes," says Anne. "Genevieve's been over there for a birthday party. They live over on Elder."

Brett writes all this down on a pad and goes out.

Anne puts her hand on Mrs. St. John's. "Did you see her?"

"I think so," she says. She stares down hard at the T-shirt, then hands it to Albers. "I think that I did."

"Where was she?"

"What did she say?"

"What did she say?" says Mrs. St. John. She touches her hair, rearranges it. "I don't know what she said. I don't know."

One nurse hands Shelley a small cup of juice. A second examines her arm where the IV line is attached. They go out.

Shelley puts the juice on the table beside her.

Exley stands up. "The only thing they can calculate now, all they can promise us, is really what's probable."

Shelley is silent.

Exley takes out a cigarette, lights it, looks around the room for an ashtray. He goes into the bathroom, takes a glass off the sink, comes back out and sits down.

Shelley is silent.

The noise, very sudden, of colliding steel carts, clattering silverware, plastic trays hitting tile floor. Shelley jumps.

Exley curses and looks toward the door.

Shelley just stares out the window; her irises flutter and vibrate.

616 ELDER LANE: the large blue house next door to the Boorstins'. It is surrounded at various distances—behind cars and trees, up on rooftops, from across the street on a church—by an FBI tactical unit. The rest of the street is blocked off by squad cars and barricades.

"Albers call in yet?" says Andrewjewski. The car he is in is parked at the end of the driveway.

"He did, sir," says the agent who sits in the driver's seat. "Young boy answered the phone, about thirteen or fourteen. Said his mother was out at some meeting."

"*Some* meeting?"

"That's what he said, sir. Some meeting."

Andrewjewski looks up at the house. All of the shades are pulled up, the curtains drawn back. A birdhouse hangs from a hook near the end of the porch.

A marksman on the roof of another house sights the back door.

Andrewjewski gets out of the car and walks up the driveway, alone. He goes up the steps to the porch, turns, then presses the doorbell.

He waits.

Three marksmen's rifles are trained on the doorway.

Andrewjewski continues to wait.

A twelve-year-old boy opens the door, zipping his pants up, holding back a frantic chihuahua with the side of his foot. He says something to Andrewjewski, then looks out beyond him.

Andrewjewski shows the boy his identification.

Still staring out at the scene in the street, the boy nudges the dog back and opens the door. The chihuahua continues to bark.

Andrewjewski turns back toward the street and touches the top of his head.

He goes into the house.

TIARNAHAN CLENCHES HIS JAW and breathes out, grinding his teeth to release the pressure inside his sinuses, as the plane drops another three hundred feet. The seat belt and no-smoking signs both light up.

He looks out the window and watches the end of the wing tilt and cut through the cloud cover. A stream of clear water sprays back off the jet.

A stewardess comes down the aisle, picking up cups, trays, and napkins, chewing gum. Tiarnahan fingers the latch on his briefcase.

The plane drops again and the lower end of Manhattan suddenly comes into view. Tiarnahan rests the side of his head on the window and stares at the Statue of Liberty.

Farther north and still lower: the Empire State Building. Central Park. It is raining.

He puts out his cigarette.

Cabs, specks of yellow, become visible now, moving between the dark buildings. The captain's voice comes over the speakers to announce what the weather will be.

Harlem. The Bronx. The East River. Trucks are now distinguishable from buses. The Hudson winds north. The horizon.

He sits back and closes his eyes, and keeps them closed for some time.

The cabin tips right as the plane, still descending over New Jersey in stages, begins circling down toward La Guardia.

He pinches his nose now, breathing out, watching Manhattan swing sideways away from him, the water gets closer and closer.

ANDREWJEWSKI walks into the study. "There's some news here now, Jack." He sits down on one of the chairs. "So I'm glad you came back." He looks at his watch. "Although it's probably nothing."

Exley stands up.

"And Shelley's okay?"

"Shelley's okay. What's the news?"

"There's been a girl, Jack, about Elizabeth's age . . . blond—"

"Alive?"

"Somebody found her—"

"Elizabeth."

"No. The body was found on the south side this afternoon in one of the forest preserves."

Exley's lips press together; he sniffs, looks away. Andrewjewski watches him closely.

"But it . . . and you're certain it isn't Elizabeth."

"It probably isn't, Jack. That's, which is the first thing we all want you and Shelley to know, that eventually, that we really don't think it's your daughter."

"But she looks like . . . I mean—"

"We've already sent three pictures of Elizabeth down there."

"And?"

"And they still can't be positive."

"Jesus . . . Where is she?"

"We hate to put you through something like this, Jack. We've just got to make sure."

"I understand that. But shit . . . So where is she?"

"They've taken her to the medical examiner's office. We'd like you to go down there and, you know, take a look at this girl. Just to be certain."

"Just to be certain. You mean . . . so you mean at the morgue?"

"They just took her in there in the last half hour or so."

"So that, so when would we be going down there?"

"Right away. We've got a helicopter and . . . whenever you're ready. I mean, I really do think that this is the easiest—"

"Let's go then."

"Because at this stage I don't believe telling Shelley . . ."

Exley nods.

"It would just—"

"Right," says Exley, shaking his head. "Neither do I."

"Basement, crawl space, the attic, garage, the upstairs . . . everywhere."

"Nothing?"

"Not shit."

"Well, the medium, you know, or whatever you call her—"

"Sure. Turned out to be about as useful's the rest of the media."

"That's beside the point, though, is it not?"

"Dragged thirty-six people along on that crapshoot. I'll give you beside the point. Whole hard-ass federal SWAT team, half of the local cops. Scared living shit outta the neighbors, not to mention—"

"We've *got* to pursue these things, though."

"Yeah, right."

"We've got to."

"Tell me about it."

"We've got to."

TIARNAHAN'S CAB moves haltingly across Forty-seventh Street, slows down, and stops. The driver starts honking.

Three car-lengths ahead of them two huge men in shirt sleeves are unloading a van in the downpour, taking their time, laughing at a joke one has told.

Tiarnahan puts his index finger into his ear, turns it, shakes his head slightly. The meter clicks ahead to $12.80.

Someone honks.

The cab moves forward again as one of the cars in front of them manages to get past the van. The driver says something in Farsi, then groans.

They slow down and stop.

They move forward, slow down, and stop.

THE TORQUE FROM the thirteen-foot props on the silver and black NCI helicopter whips the bushes and trees into a frenzy in the Rawlses' backyard as Exley and Brett climb in back of the pilot.

A minicam operator leans out of NewsChopper5 and begins shooting this scene from the air.

The NCI helicopter rises straight up, hovers at treetop level for two or three seconds, then swings out over the lake. It is followed by NewsChopper5.

Exley looks down. He looks scared.

Both helicopters cut back over Kenilworth now, picking up speed, and head south-southwest toward the city.

TIARNAHAN HANDS the driver a twenty, gets out of the cab, and dashes across the wide sidewalk, dodging pedestrians and covering his head with his briefcase, then pushes his way through the revolving glass door of the Forty-seventh Street entrance of 580 Fifth Avenue.

The lobby is packed. Nearly all of the men wear black suits, black ties, black coats, and *shtreimels;* their beards hang down past their collars. Tall black guards, with badges and holstered revolvers, are positioned in various corners. There are not any women. Tiarnahan watches himself for a second or two in one of the fifteen TV monitors as he stands by the building's directory.

There's also a camera in the elevator car he goes up in. To his left is a man who's at most four feet tall. What hair there is on his head is clipped short, but his curly brown beard hangs down onto his chest; several long strands from the beard near his temple have been pulled up and back, along with the curved silver frames of his glasses, and hang down in back of his ear. Beside this man there's another man—also bearded, also dressed all in black—who's six feet seven or eight. The two men speak softly in Yiddish.

Tiarnahan excuses himself and gets out at the seventeenth floor. A guard glances up from his desk, looks him over, then goes back to reading the *Post*.

The hallway is narrow and long, dimly lit. Each door is marked with a four-digit number in brass and a plaque bearing the name of the company inside. Tiarnahan finds room 1720—the third to last door on the right—and goes in.

The wall facing the entrance in the tiny reception area has a gray metal door and beside it a teller's window shielded with bulletproof glass. Tiarnahan waits, presses a button, and waits.

A young red-haired woman appears on the other side of the glass and says "Yes?"

Tiarnahan passes his card under the glass through the curved metal slot at the bottom. "I have an appointment with Mr. Broch."

The woman looks at the card then down at the calendar page on her desk. Tiarnahan smiles.

The woman points in the direction of the gray metal door and presses a loud, rasping buzzer.

The walnut-paneled viewing room of the Cook County Medical Examiner's Office. Exley, Brett, and Chief Deputy Examiner Henry F. Carr are standing alongside a brown naugahyde sofa. A black-and-white TV monitor hangs from a strut in the corner; its picture, rolling vertically once every two or three seconds, is badly distorted by feedback and static.

Carr curses under his breath, turns some more knobs on the side of the monitor, apologizes. "Looks like we're gonna have to take you downstairs."

"What's downstairs?" Exley says.

"What we're trying to show you up here," says Carr. To Brett: "The corpus delicti."

Exley sits down; he stares at the shiny brown arm of the sofa.

"Please. Right this way."

They leave the viewing room, make two right turns, go down a short flight of steps.

"Cause of death," says Carr, "is still pending toxicological study."

As they go down the next flight—this one much longer—the stairwell begins to be filled with the sharp sweetgray odor of decomposition. Neither Brett nor Exley acknowledges this.

"One of the intake clerks will bring her over to where you can see her."

Brett and Exley are silent. The odor gets stronger as they continue to go down the steps.

At the bottom of the third flight the stairwell is blocked by a dull black steel door; a two-foot-square panel of reinforced Plexiglas has been placed in the middle. Above this door is a sign: NO ADMITTANCE.

Carr knocks twice on the glass. Brett puts his hand on Exley's left shoulder.

He removes it.

Fifteen seconds later a young black intake clerk wheels a long sideless cart up to the other side of the door, passing in front of it and stopping when the left end of the cart is directly in front of the window. He stares out at Carr through the glass.

The forty-four-inch body on top of the cart is covered with a black plastic sheet. Exley stares down at the bulge that is formed by the head.

Carr looks over at Exley, then turns and nods to the clerk.

Exley stares down at the sheet.

The clerk takes the end of the sheet with both hands and raises it back off the head. Exley's teeth grind together and he breathes out hard through his mouth. His eyes remain open.

Brett looks over at Exley, then down.

Exley begins to say something, can't. He just looks.

The neck has been wrenched slightly sideways so the head faces straight up at Exley. The light brown hair is matted and tangled, both eyes are frozen half open, the lips are light blue. On the side of the chin there's a bruise.

Brett puts his hand on Exley's shoulder again. Carr is silent.

Exley puts his hand on the Plexiglas.

He closes his eyes.

A PAIR OF PORTABLE blackboards have been set up in the living room in front of the Jeanette Pasin Sloan canvas. On the smaller, light green one—the one on the right—has been written:

$$\lim_{k \to \infty} A^{3k} = \lim_{k \to \infty} \begin{pmatrix} (A_{13}A_{32}A_{21})^k & 0 & 0 \\ 0 & (A_{21}A_{13}A_{32})^k & 0 \\ 0 & 0 & (A_{32}A_{21}A_{13})^k \end{pmatrix}$$

"But so—"

"So you figure—"

"I'm afraid I don't follow."

"This is just an example," says Andrewjewski.

"I mean—"

"In other words, you can never really get the whole story."

"You got it," says Finn.

"Ex*act*ly."

"If you don't mind, gentlemen—"

"Jesus."

"Let's all back up just a bit."

Andrewjewski writes on the larger—black—blackboard:

$$\sum_{j=1}^{n} a_{ij} w_j / w_i = n \qquad i = 1, \ldots, n$$

"Wonderful."

"Please, guys..."

"Just listen," says Andrewjewski. "On the right side here, right here, is the same constant, n, the largest possible eigenvalue of A. The other eigenvalues all equal zero. So, since the rank of A must be unity, and the sum, the sum of the eigenvalues is equal to—"

He writes:

$$\sum a_{ii} = n$$

Luz brings a tray of sandwiches into the room, looks at the boards, begins to pass out the sandwiches.

"So what Jim's doing, what we're trying to avoid here, is sliding into the usual zero-sum impasse."

"Exactly."

"Even if the big decision's already been made?"

"We've got to be prepared for every possible contingency."

"So that when the deductive process, the process gets—"

"Come again?"

"Thank you."

"We assign these eigenvalues for pair-comparison judgments only. It's really quite simple. All we're doing is asking ourselves two simple questions: Which of two alternatives is the more significant or better, and, second, what is the magnitude of the difference?"

"Right."

Luz passes again in front of the boards and goes out.

"We try, you see, we try to let the figures we come up with reflect as accurately as possible our feelings, our considered opinions, but at the same time allowing for a moderate amount of uncertainty."

"What if we disagree on—"

"We just average them. And if we err at all, we always want to be sure—"

"*Which* figures, though?"

"What happened to the good old days with the X's and cosines?"

"These," says Andrewjewski. He writes:

INTENSITY	
1	activities of equal importance
3	inconclusive evidence favoring one activity
5	good evidence—logical criteria favoring . . .
7	conclusive evidence . . .
9	absolute—maximum poss. ev . . .

"We've already got this stuff down on the sheet."

"Right," says Andrewjewski.

Then, down in the corner of the same board, he writes:

$$a_{ij} = w_i/w_j$$

"What we compare, then, is the ith activity—"

"Right—"

"—with the jth."

"Got it."

"You follow?"

"*Oh* yeah."

"Suuure."

There is laughter.

"What could be simpler."

Rawls takes a bite of his sandwich.

"What about the kth with the lth? Can you—"

"Would you mind running that last part by us again?"

Andrewjewski loosens his tie, brushes some chalk dust off his pants, and says "Sure."

"Contractions," says Shelley. "That's pretty much what they feel like. Contractions."

Dr. Traisman feels Shelley's abdomen, squeezes it gently, looks down into her eyes.

Shelley reaches down and touches the lower part of her side, presses one spot, then moves her hand back and forth. "They're all in through here."

"Feeling cold at all too?"

"Chills," she says. "Just when—"

"When the pressure begins to start up again?"

"Yes."

A nurse, standing on the other side of the bed, says, "She's been soaking through her peripads. Almost two an hour."

Traisman nods.

Shelley winces then and closes her eyes.

"What we're going to do," says Traisman. He covers her up now and waits for the contraction to pass.

The nurse takes Shelley's bedpan and leaves.

"Is increase the Tributaline to help take some of this pressure off of your uterus."

Shelley doesn't respond.

"The most important thing now, I think, is for you to try to relax."

"I really..."

"Otherwise," says Traisman, "how are you doing?"

Shelley breathes out hard through her mouth and looks up.

She breathes in.

F‌RANK FINN CRUISES slowly past the end of the Rawlses' driveway on Sheridan Road, heading north, announcing through his squad car's overhead speaker that all members of the press—everyone, in fact—is to vacate the area immediately.

Many of the reporters—most now have copies of the official directive—have already begun to disperse.

Other policemen move on foot through the crowd, passing out more of the copies.

A scuffle breaks out for a second or two between one of the Cook County sheriffs and the members of a minicam crew.

Still and video cameramen shoot the policemen who continue to pass out the copies.

By Frank Finn's sixth pass, most of reporters have begun to walk up the block to their cars.

"Warms the cockles of my heart."
"As it stands now we've got a simple Hobbs Act violation."
"But it's making the Exley girl that much more vulnerable."
"Although that Kissinger business—"
"The '73 Kissinger policy doesn't even apply here."
"One man's terrorist, you know . . ."
"Reality's just out of their depth."
"Exactly."
"Because this isn't just some sort of crapshoot."
"It's not, huh."
"And the business about Rawls's culpability's about as bogus a—"
"What you call polytetrafluoroethylene logic."
"Say what?"
"Look it up."
"Don't have to. It's—"
"Tell me about it. It's what?"
"It's Gaelic for real fucking slippery."

A̲ndrewjewski, doodling on the back of an envelope, nodding, speaking into the telephone. "Daytime," he says. "Yes ... the woman ... the young woman on Tower."

He traces the right-angled lines of a four six or eight times, shakes his head and says yes, then completes the figure by crossing it with a vertical line several times.

"Exley's not back yet."

He listens, underlining the four with his pen.

"I hope so," he says. "Very good."

He hangs up the phone.

"Anyway," he says. He puts down his pen. "Our tracing capabilities aren't what most people think they are."

Rawls only nods.

"We'll set up a prearranged code for you. You express your cooperation, your willingness to, and keep asking them questions to draw out the length of the call. Try to calm the guy down and get some sort of proof that it's—"

"Be obsequious."

"Right. Just about, just this side of obsequious. The tapes will get background noise, voiceprint characteristics ... if we're lucky. What *you've* got to do is convince him that nothing good happens for them until *we* get the girl back. Under no—"

"Right."

"Right."

"Yeah. You know, the first thing I wanted to ask the guy, what I still want to know was, is what if I hadn't got that letter on Monday. I mean, even with the special delivery, I could just as easily gone off to work this morning . . . I was even thinking we could use something like that to stall them and—"

"I thought about that. The problem's that, what was Exley doing over here, then, talking to you?"

"Right."

"Anyway, look at this," says Andrewjewski. He holds up a black leather pouch. "There's a very thin silicon diode transmitter sewn inside this seam here, right along here . . ."

"The diamonds go into the pouch . . ."

"We hand over the diamonds . . ."

They are silent.

"And they take the diamonds home with them."

Rawls only nods.

"At which point . . ."

"I hope so."

"It becomes merely a matter of time."

They are silent.

"I hope so."

Two reporters—a woman wearing a gray flannel business suit and medium heels, a man in a brown leather jacket and blue jeans—rush out the door of the Tribune Tower in downtown Chicago and head north on Michigan Avenue.

They alternate jogging and walking—mostly the latter—picking their way through the crowd on the sidewalks, helping each other along, making about the same time as the buses and cabs in the street.

The woman looks at her watch as they pass Saks Fifth Avenue. They pick up the pace.

They go by the WAIT Radio Building, then get stopped by a red light at Huron.

At Chicago Avenue they stop again and speak to each other, the man holding on to the woman's left elbow, waiting for the light to turn green. Two men in mohawks wait with them.

They pass the old water tower. The woman's ankle turns on her heel now, but she regains her balance, unhurt. The man slows down and waits up for her.

They go in the main entrance of Water Tower Place and stop, out of breath. The woman takes a small red tablet from out of her pocket, opens it, refers to some note. They both walk quickly then toward the escalator.

They mount the stairs of the escalator, moving past several people, until halfway up they are stopped by a tiny couple in their seventies standing shoulder to shoulder on one of the stairs. They ride the rest of the way up standing still.

They take another escalator from the second floor to the third—moving more freely now, quicker—and another from the third to the fourth.

They end up on the fifth floor in front of F.A.O. Schwarz. The woman refers to the tablet again. They speak to each other. The man looks around, then points to a pair of unenclosed phone booths in the small corridor behind them that leads to the women's and men's rooms.

Neither of the phones is in use. The woman pauses, then moves to the phone on the right. She reaches behind the large black metal-bound Yellow Pages, looks at the man, then pulls out the blue outer wrapper of an empty pack of Freedent peppermint gum; it is rolled up to about the size of a cigarette butt.

The woman weighs the pack on her palm, holding it up to the man. They look at each other.

HALTINGLY, through the shadows and dusk, its spotlights flooding the leaves and the grass, a Chicago Police Department helicopter lands in Rawls's backyard. The racket is deafening.

Andrewjewski looks at his watch. It is 4:44.

Andrewjewski and Rawls approach as the racket subsides. Exley stands back.

Tiarnahan gets out of the helicopter, shakes Rawls's hand, hands him the brown leather briefcase.

Andrewjewski turns, points his large fist at Exley, puts up his thumb.

N INETY-NINE DIAMONDS, in the fluorescent light from the desk lamp, in a pile on Rawls's taupe desk blotter. To the left of the pile the brown leather briefcase, to the right the black leather pouch.

Luz comes in with a tray. Ignoring the diamonds, she hands glasses of milk to Exley and Rawls, to Andrewjewski a glass of iced tea. "Ice machine still no working, Mr. Rawls."

"That's all right, Luz. Thanks."

"Should I order in the morning more ice?"

"Probably be a good idea. Yes."

Exley looks at his watch. It is 5:55.

Luz goes out.

The diamonds. Beyond them, the row of gray phones.

"Jesus," says Exley. He takes out a cigarette.

Rawls just stares at the glass in his hand.

Andrewjewski loosens the drawstring, opens the pouch, begins dropping the diamonds in seven or eight at a time.

Rawls takes a sip of his milk.

EXLEY AND TRAISMAN, over the telephone, quietly:
"But we're giving her something to help calm her down and something to take off that pressure. She may even be sleeping already."
"Yeah. I heard all about it."
A silence.
"Last time I talked to her she made the announcement. You know, told me—"
"Jack, I can promise you—"
"Although you really couldn't expect her to be exactly slaphappy."
A silence.
"Now could you."
A silence.
"Maybe phasing oneself out at this point isn't all that bad an idea."
A silence.
"Just kidding, of course, Doctor. Just babbling."
"She's gonna be fine, Jack. We're watching her here very closely."
"There any way, by the way, not to change the subject,

but there any way our having had intercourse Sunday night could've—"

"No way, Jack. Not at this stage. No way."

"Just wanted to know."

"No way, Jack. Believe me."

A silence.

"One other thing, Jack, something I've been meaning to ask you ... Where are Shelley's mother and father? I mean, are they—"

"It's really probably better if we didn't go into that now. Just believe me that you don't want to know."

"Fine, Jack. Whatever."

A silence.

"Well, then. Good luck."

"And so you have this number."

"Okay."

A silence.

"Okay, then."

"I'll call you."

ANDREWJEWSKI, alone, in Rawls's study, holding the blue Freedent gum packet.

He finally unrolls it, turns it upside down, shakes it. A child's white incisor falls out onto the desk blotter; its minuscule roots are stained with dry blood.

Andrewjewski stares at the tooth for a while, massaging his temples, then stands.

He picks up the tooth, turns it around in his fingers, looks at the door. Then he drops the tooth into the packet and rolls it back up.

He glances around the small room—at the bookshelves, the painting, the tape deck, the ashtrays, the row of gray phones—coughs, clears his throat.

He carefully wraps the packet in a sheet of blank looseleaf, then puts it inside his coat pocket.

"But there are still certain things, no matter what, that just can't be measured. It's simply the nature—"

"Not with the crapshoot you've got going down around here."

"You guys hear what one of those broad reporters this afternoon started asking? Wanted to know what SOAR stood for."

"Sisters Organized in Amazon Rage."

"Who said that. You?"

"Shit no. *She* did."

"That's what she said. Said 'Well isn't that what it stands for?' "

"You see that pile of diamonds in there?"

"I'll give the sebaceous bitch *organ*ized."

"Said it cost Rawls, cost somebody, seven and three quarter mil."

"Should've pawned off those industrial stones on them like they were planning to."

"Real good thinking. And you've got two small kids of your own."

"Or used carbonados."

"Right."

"Carbonados are black, genius. They don't even *look* like real diamonds."

"You guys are too fucking much. Do you know that?"

"What? You learn that down there at that school of yours?"

"That's right, dickfor. Where'd *you* go to school?"

"Spent the whole time down there plunking his glockenspiel."

"You got it."

"Organized in Amazon rage."

"Yeah right. Your only problem's that you've got this very small particle of brain lodged somewhere inside your skull."

"Tell me about it."

"Well, you see, it's like this . . ."

RAWLS COMES INTO his study carrying a *Tribune,* some folders, a pear. Exley is standing in front of the bookshelves, head cocked to one side, reading titles. Andrewjewski sits on the couch, knees pressed together, writing on a small yellow pad.

There is silence.

Rawls looks at his watch—it is 8:48—then places the folders and pear on top of a file cabinet.

There is silence.

Exley pulls a thin blue hardcover book halfway out of the shelf. "Is this—"

The telephone rings; it's the second phone from the left. Andrewjewski gets up off the couch, clicks on the tape deck, and answers it. "Rawls residence."

Exley looks over at Rawls.

"Yes . . . May I ask who is calling?"

Rawls starts scratching his cheekbone.

"All right. He's . . . yes."

Andrewjewski hands Rawls the phone.

"Hello."

Andrewjewski puts on the headphones and listens.

Shifting his weight from foot to foot, blinking, Exley just watches.

"Yes," says Rawls. "Yes, I do have—have them . . . Yes." He looks at Andrewjewski. "Ah hah . . . I'm listening. But we'd also like to ask *you* something . . . Yes. But how do I know—"

Rawls stares at Andrewjewski, at Exley, listens hard into the phone. "We got cut off."

"He hung up," says Andrewjewski. He takes off the headphones.

"What?" Exley says.

"He just hung up," says Rawls. "I was just asking him how we'd be able to, that Elizabeth . . ."

Exley pivots toward Rawls and throws a wild roundhouse right. Rawls starts to duck, but the blow still catches his cheekbone, knocking him sideways, backward, and down. Meantime Andrewjewski has put his shoulder into Exley's chest and driven him back onto the couch. Exley cries out and covers his ribs with his forearm.

Rawls makes it up on one knee. "Jesus H. fucking Christ."

The telephone receiver still lies on the carpet. The tape deck continues to turn.

Andrewjewski disengages himself from Exley and gets back up off the couch. "Jack, listen—"

Rawls stands up.

"How could you do that," says Exley, to Rawls. "I mean I'm sorry I—but how could you fucking *do* that?"

"Do what?" says Rawls.

Exley leans forward, catching his breath, still holding on to his ribs.

"I mean Christ, Jack," says Rawls.

"Do what."

"They'll call back, Jack," says Andrewjewski. He bends down and hangs up the phone.

There is silence.

"Whatever you said," Exley says. He rubs his right knuckles. "Fucking *whatever* it is that you said."

A DARK-COLORED squad car moves down a street with its lights off.

Its windows are rolled all the way up, but disembodied voices can still be made out through the glass and the static, squawking out over the radio.

The driver is smoking a cigarette.

EXLEY AND BRETT. Rawls's porch. Exley is holding his shoe.

"Both of us, I guess," Exley says. He turns his shoe upside down and shakes out a pebble. "We apologized."

Brett only nods.

Exley gets down on one knee, pulls on his shoe, starts to tie it. "It's just that, nothing happens. I'm getting to feel like the Karen Ann Quinlan of fathers."

He stands up.

"That doctor called back," says Brett. "Reminded you to keep taking those pills."

"What we'd all better do is get ready to have Elizabeth stay dead a long time."
"Doing what?"
"It's a fuck job, but still."
"Yeah. But guess what."
"What."
"I kind of do not want to hear about it."

"I MEAN PHYSICALLY," says Exley. He's back in the study. "You know what I feel like?"

Andrewjewski just waits for the answer.

"It's like I felt when I tried to quit smoking. Seeing tracers, dizzy, and there's this vague sort of aura all in here through my muscles."

"Like a daze of some sort."

Exley massages his forearm. "The thing with my rib, plus I've got this taste in my mouth . . ."

On the coffee table between them there's a clear plastic bag with some ice in it. What's left of one of the cubes melts off and falls now, collapsing that part of the pile.

Andrewjewski gets up and turns on the tape deck. He lets it whine in reverse for five or six seconds, clicks on fast forward, then stops it.

They listen.

Silence. Click.

ANDREWJEWSKI: *Rawls residence.*
MALE VOICE: *Burke Rawls there please?*
ANDREWJEWSKI: *Yes.*
MALE VOICE: *May I speak with him please?*

Unintelligible whispering.

ANDREWJEWSKI: *May I ask who is calling?*
MALE VOICE: *No, you may not. Just put Burke Rawls on and don't waste my time.*
ANDREWJEWSKI: *All right. He's—*
MALE VOICE: *Is he there?*
Unintelligible whispering.
ANDREWJEWSKI: *Yes.*
Silence.
Unintelligible whispering.
RAWLS: *Hello.*
Exley lights a cigarette.
MALE VOICE: *Do you have them?*
RAWLS: *Yes.*
MALE VOICE: *The diamonds.*
RAWLS: *Yes, I do have them.*
MALE VOICE: *All of them, the specified quality . . .*
RAWLS: *Yes.*
Unintelligible whispering.
RAWLS: *Ah hah.*
MALE VOICE: *All right, then. You read what we said, Burke, so prick up your ears now . . .*
RAWLS: *I'm listening. But we'd also like to ask you something now.*
Unintelligible whispering.
MALE VOICE: *No you don't, Burke. Just shut up and listen. You got that?*
Unintelligible whispering.
RAWLS: *Yes. But how do I know—*
Bang and click of the receiver.
A dial tone.
RAWLS: *We got cut off.*
ANDREWJEWSKI (farther off): *He hung up.*
EXLEY (farther off): *What?*

RAWLS: *He just hung up. I was just asking him how we'd be able to, that Elizabeth—*
 Shuffling noise, then a clap. The receiver bangs, vibrating loudly, onto the floor, then bounces around. Scuffling noise. A thud, then the floor trembles. A cry, farther off. Silence.
RAWLS: *Jesus H. fucking Christ.*
Silence.
 "Expletive deleted," says Exley.
 "Right."
ANDREWJEWSKI: *Jack listen—*
EXLEY (out of breath): *How could you do that. I mean I'm sorry I—but how could you fucking do that.*
RAWLS: *Do what?*
Silence.
RAWLS: *I mean Christ, Jack.*
EXLEY: *Do what?*
ANDREWJEWSKI: *They'll call back, Jack.*
Silence.
 Footsteps. Click of the receiver.

 They sit there in silence—Exley still on the small leather couch, Andrewjewski in Rawls's desk chair—watching the silent tape move from one reel to the other. A haze of cigarette smoke floats in the light near the ceiling.
 "I'm going out," says Exley. He puts out his cigarette.
 "Sounds like a good idea," says Andrewjewski. He shuts off the tape deck. "I'll be right here."
 "Just take a short walk out back," Exley says. He looks out the window into the darkness. "Get some air."
 Andrewjewski shifts his weight in the chair. "Good." He nods. "Do."

They are silent.
"And so, so you'll be in here."
"You go ahead," says Andrewjewski. "Don't worry."
Exley nods.
They both remain seated, staring off past one another.

NEWSCHOPPER 5 swings past the thin slice of moon.

The moon reflects down off the lake.

NewsChopper5 reappears, swinging back past the reflection.

1:14 WEDNESDAY MORNING.

Rawls, in a clay-colored jacket, is alone at his desk reading *Forbes*. One of the phones with his name on it lights up and rings. He sits up straight, puts down the magazine, blinks. His cheekbone is swollen and purple. The phone rings a second time.

He looks out the door, listens, starts snapping his fingers. He waits.

The phone rings a third time.

He picks it up finally, clears his throat, glances again toward the door. "Hello?"

Brett rushes into the study.

Rawls is now standing. He nods energetically at Brett and says yes while pointing into the receiver. "And I'm sorry . . ." He continues to nod and to point. "Yes, we do."

Brett rushes out.

"I do," says Rawls. He leans across the top of his desk and pushes a lever on the side of the tape deck. "What you do . . ."

The reels start to move in reverse. "I hope so."

He pushes a second lever, stopping the reels. "Yes . . . but just . . ." He grabs a red pen and starts writing—scribbling actually—on the desk blotter. "Yes."

Brett, Andrewjewski, and Exley come in; having been outside, Andrewjewski and Exley's faces are pink.

Rawls continues to scribble, nodding, nodding, underlining two of the words. "Never . . . no . . . no . . . never mind."

Andrewjewski looks down, realizes the deck isn't on, hits record. Exley exhales.

Rawls continues to write as he talks. "Do. Yes . . . it's very . . . they are."

Andrewjewski takes off his jacket and looks over at Brett. Brett looks at Exley.

"Got it," says Rawls. He sits down. "Yes . . . yeah . . . of course not." He looks up at Exley. "Right . . . okay . . . sure. Sure. But let me read all that back to you . . ." He looks up at Andrewjewski and winces.

"Hung up?"

"Yup."

"Well?" says Exley.

"Jesus," says Rawls. He hangs up the phone. "All right. I've got it. I wrote it all down."

"Good," says Andrewjewski. He turns off the tape deck. "I tried to be obsequious as hell."

"Is Elizabeth there," Exley says. "Did you talk to her."

"You did a good job."

"I didn't get to talk to her, no. You're the one, by the way," says Rawls. He points to the blotter. "It's, you're the one they want to hand over the diamonds."

"But they're supposed—"

"I'm . . . you mean now?"

"I guess so."

"I'm ready," says Exley. "I'm ready."

Andrewjewski wants to know "What did they actually say?"

"Listen," says Rawls. "Here's what he said." He refers to the blotter. "They want Exley, Jack, Jack's to deliver the diamonds." He looks up at Exley. "You're supposed to be wearing a, let's see, a stocking cap and a light-colored jacket and be, to be walking south on the east—"

"But I don't—"

"We'll *get* you one, Jack. Don't—"

"Look," says Rawls. "Listen. I've got one I think you might, out in the closet. The important thing is that they want you to be alone. All alone. He came down on that hard, said it three or four times." He looks at the blotter again. "You walk south on Sheridan till you come to the phone booth at the corner of Elder." To Andrewjewski: "Said he'd receive further *tutelage* when he gets there."

"When. That's good, Burke. But when."

"Right away I assume. Soon as—"

"I mean, what time."

"They, *shit*. He didn't say. They actually didn't *say* what time I don't think."

"*What?*" Exley says.

"Jesus."

"What time is it now?"

"You're sure, Burke."

"One-seventeen."

"I'm positive."

"They must've meant right away, though."

"The corner of Elder and Sheridan."

"Right."

Andrewjewski glances at Brett, nods, looks back at Rawls. Brett goes out.

"Okay," Exley says. "That is good."

"Your jacket right there," says Andrewjewski, to Rawls. "Let me see it a second."

Rawls takes off his jacket, hands it to Andrewjewski.

"What we've got to make sure," says Exley. "What you don't—"

"It's gonna work out, Jack. Don't worry."

Andrewjewski looks over the jacket—at the same time palming a small metal disk, which he ends up dropping into one of the pockets—then hands it to Exley.

"What they said was a light-colored jacket," says Exley. "Wasn't that what they said?"

"You don't think this is light enough."

Exley holds the jacket up to the light. "Is this what you'd really call light-colored?"

"It's tan. Or it's clay-colored."

"It's a light-colored jacket, Jack. Believe me."

"Don't worry about it. Really, it's fine."

Brett comes back in now. He immediately starts pressing buttons on one of the phones.

Exley takes off his own jacket, throws it onto the couch, puts on Rawls's. It fits.

"And you do have a stocking cap," says Andrewjewski.

"Right," says Rawls. "Right out here."

Rawls goes toward the door. As he steps past Exley, a man wearing tan corduroy pants, a navy-blue jacket, gloves, and a ski mask pulled down over his face walks into the study. "Good evening," he says. "Call me Ed."

Brett hangs up the phone and draws out a pistol; the man just ignores it.

"Mr. Exley?" he says, facing Exley.

"Right."

The man moves to the windows and signals to someone outside. He turns then and looks at Andrewjewski. "May I ask who's quarterbacking this operation?"

A telephone rings.

"I am," says Andrewjewski.

"That's for you, then."

"The first thing we'd like to know," says Andrewjewski, "is—"

The man looks at Exley. "It's your daughter."

Andrewjewski picks up the phone.

"What I'd like to do," says the man. He looks now at Rawls. "What I'd sort of like to do now is use your good offices here—"

"Yes, I would," says Andrewjewski. "Provided of course that we see . . . no . . . put her on, then."

"To so to speak extricate ourselves," says the man, "from our predicament."

Andrewjewski says "Andrewjewski . . . yes. Put her on."

"My colleagues, by the way, are just outside in the driveway," says the man. He looks right at Brett. "So please remind your friends that if anything *untoward* should happen out there, Miss Elizabeth is going to have one kingsize problem."

Brett just stares back at him.

"Go tell them," says Exley. "Come on."

"Yes," says Andrewjewski. "Although who's . . . *yes* . . . yes. Ed is here."

"Jesus," says Rawls.

Andrewjewski signals for Brett to go out, then reaches over—keeping his eyes on the man—and hands Exley the phone. "She's fine," he says. "It's Elizabeth."

Brett leaves the room with his pistol.

"Yup," says the man. His eyes are light blue. "One *heck* of a king-size problem."

"Honey?" says Exley. "It's Daddy . . . yes." His voice goes up an octave and cracks. "I'm right here now."

The man glances around the study. "Very tasteful," he says "*Very* tasteful. May I ask where're the diamonds?"

Rawls points them out.

221

"Ah."

"Sure," Exley says. "And we're gonna see you real soon, E. Really soon . . . Your tooth? . . . Can you hear me? . . . Right . . . yeah, I'm real tired too."

The man takes a brown paper bag from his pocket, unfolds it, and carefully pours the diamonds from the pouch to the bag.

"Who's this?" Exley says.

Andrewjewski and Rawls exchange glances.

"Don't worry," says Exley. "Right . . . I won't. And you have my . . . yeah. Should . . . but should I . . . got it." He hands Andrewjewski the phone.

"What."

"I do not want," says Exley. "You simply absolutely cannot follow them out of here."

Andrewjewski listens into the phone, looks at the man, and hangs up.

"It's the most important part of the deal," Exley says. "They explicitly promised that if they see any cars, helicopters, anything suspicious at all they would kill her."

"The man's got a point," says the man. He looks out the window.

"*The* point," says Rawls.

The man holds the bag up to Rawls in a kind of salute, bows, then stuffs the bag into his pocket.

Andrewjewski stares hard at the man. "We're not gonna follow them, Jack."

"And you have what you came for, my friend," says Rawls. "Just understand that we want that girl back now."

The man puts up his right hand. "You have my word."

"Understand?"

"She better come back," Exley says. He grabs the man's sleeve.

"Jack, relax!"

He lets go. "What are you planning to do?"

"Leave," says the man. To Andrewjewski: "Is everything clear?"

"Everything is perfectly clear," says Andrewjewski. "You're free to go now."

"Right," says the man. "The problem's that I never needed someone like you, old boy, to tell me these things."

"Whatever you say," says Andrewjewski. "I assure you we're all most impressed."

"As well you might be."

"When," Exley says. "We'd like to know when she'll, exactly when you plan to release her."

"As a matter of fact, you're gonna get your kid back real soon."

"When."

A horn honks outside.

"Gotta go," says the man. "If there's any funny business at all when we start to drive out of here"—he raises his index finger—"I give you my word that she gets it."

"I mean it," says Exley. "I'd follow you till I drop in my tracks."

"Just go," says Andrewjewski. "You know what we want and we intend to see you deliver."

The man begins to walk out. "This has been a delicate business," he says. "Wouldn't you say? And I want you to know that I think you've all comported yourselves rather admirably."

The man leaves the study. The other four follow.

As they walk through the living room one of the phones rings again. Brett hesitates, looks over at Andrewjewski, then runs back to answer it. Genevieve, Anne, and two agents look out at them now from the kitchen.

"Look at it this way," says the man. "How am I gonna look *next time* if we *don't* send her back."

No one responds.

They go out. The air frosts their breath as soon as they step out the door.

"Just keep in mind what I've said," says the man.

"And you do the same," says Andrewjewski.

A navy-blue Plymouth Reliant K is parked in the driveway; its lights are on and its motor is running. Two men in ski masks are sitting in front, looking around at the six special agents who have surrounded the car. One of the agents furiously writes on a tablet. A gray Impala is parked right up against the front of the Plymouth; a green Impala is parked right in back of it.

The man tries to shake hands with Exley, but Exley won't offer his hand. He turns then and shakes hands with Rawls.

"I'm not gonna beg you," says Exley.

"No need to, friend. I'm a man of my word."

"But if she doesn't come back, I will kill you."

"Sounds fair enough," says the man. He turns then, opens the left rear door of the Plymouth, gets in.

Brett comes out of the house now and stands next to Andrewjewski. "She said to tell Mr. Andrewjewski they are going to hurt me if you try to follow Ed's car."

The man rolls down his window. "It goes without saying . . ."

Andrewjewski signals to the other agents to allow the Reliant to pass. A strobe light goes on and one of the agents clicks off a half dozen shots with a camera. Exley blinks.

The Impala parked in front of the Reliant pulls back out of the way. The man turns and waves.

"We've got them," says Andrewjewski, to Rawls.

The Reliant moves down the long driveway; the Impalas stay right where they are. Exley watches, blinks, turns away; then he watches again. The brake lights go on when the Reliant reaches Sheridan Road, the brake lights go off, it turns right.

"I don't think so," says Rawls.

MARY EXLEY, alone on a chair in her kitchen, her legs covered up with a quilt. The faucet drips every ten or twelve seconds into one of the plates in the sink. She fingers the cross of her rosary, then stops.

The faucet now drips seven times without Mary moving.

E<small>XLEY STANDS</small> in the middle of Sheridan Road. There are no cars coming in either direction. He still has on Rawls's jacket.

He shivers.

A dim glow of headlights appear from the south now. He watches. The headlights get brighter and closer. He blinks.

The car, a Volkswagen Beetle, gets closer. Exley can make out the sound of the radio playing over the groan and tap of the engine: first the chords, then the drums, and finally the song: "Twist and Shout."

The occupants of the car do not look his way as they pass him. A plane goes by overhead. Exley can still hear the song.

He looks down.

"But which leaves us in here and Elizabeth and the diamonds out there."

"What they've got to be weighing now are the risks involved in letting her go."

"Or *not* letting her go. Because it seems to me—"

"Exactly. It just seems like it's a lot more dangerous for them now to have to deliver her anywhere, sticking their necks out like that. It would be easier for them just to kill her."

"Not to mention the fact she's a witness of sorts."

"*My* guess is that they're still very close. We know now where they got that plastique. We think we know where the typewriter's from, we think we've got one of their names, and we know where they got the two cars. We're not in bad shape."

"The problem's—"

"You think maybe they don't like what we gave them?"

"Who knows."

"They better had like it."

"Once we find them, we can call in and see what they have to say for themselves. If the girl's still alive we should still be able to work something out."

"And if not?"

"If not? . . . If not, they'll have made a serious, a fatal mistake, and we'd have them for sure. We're counting on them to keep that fact well in mind."

"Anyway . . ."

"It was simply the nature of the game they were playing to keep us in limbo."

"Yeah, but it worked. They played that beautiful."

"Once the transmitter was taken out of the picture—"

"Plus the guy showing up like that, out of the blue . . ."

"Trying to get any kind of fix then on where they were headed would've risked, you know, to the girl once we got there."

"They also could've been moving her from one spot to the other, so that while we were following the *one* car—"

"Exactly."

"We'd never've known whether they'd picked up on us till after they, until after—"

"Exactly."

"Although we're still more or less, we're still not in all that bad a shape."

BERNIE ZIGULSKI, on a waiting room couch in Evanston Hospital, lit only by Channel 9's test pattern, still in his work clothes, asleep.

SHELLEY DREAMS, shivers and dreams, can't stop her thinking.
    hears herself thinking and dreaming
    about what but what about all those my all my
    it's all all my fault all my fault she's gone now she's
    forever forever it's Jesus it's for ever I know it forever
    they just did an ultrasound
    why
    what's the point, what anything anything but this
    I'd give anything
    but I'm going I'm going I'm going to do it if   if
    if because if I hadn't sent her I just sent her
    to   all alone
    breathing
    I'm drugged drugged I'm just I know it I'm practically
    shouldn't be sleeping they gave me that never the
    the prognosis she'd never just please God please please
    what God I'm having this baby
    should have
    I can't have
    I can't see her face just can't picture
    could have done was stay home or and made her stay home E

just kept you E
kept you home
but now Jesus they're
they're both dead forever all dead now all dead if
if I'd just if only I'd
my children my two my
my dead two my dead just they're gone oh we'd just
promised I was where promised
she'd be home we all wouldn't be she'd be home
home we'd be home yes and yes please please it's
and it's soaking and and staying that way a long time
she'd be home now if only I'd
I could've stayed home with her always just always
I'm dead no
but I never just never I should never E never
have no oh no just please no no please no my baby
it's my no oh no no no I'll no my baby
No

EXLEY LIES FACEUP on the couch.

Businesslike, almost frantic activity proceeds all around him: Andrewjewski and Brett on the phones, Rawls and Lennon whispering, Anne Rawls just staring at Exley and drinking, Luz bringing in cups of coffee.

Exley turns over. He clasps his hands under his knees and faces the back of the couch. As he does, the small metal disk falls from the pocket of Rawls's clay-colored jacket and slides off the couch to the floor.

And, for the moment at least, no one notices.

A PIERCING SCREECH twists Shelley's face, ripping her mouth open, then trails off into a sob.

She trembles, shivers, opens her eyes in the darkness. Except for her sobs, there is silence.

Two nurses rush into the room.

Two policemen in puttees on horseback, several dogs, eight or ten unmarked patrol cars.

Lighted cigarettes flare and radios squawk in the darkness. No one is moving.

The dogs sniff and whimper.

Shelley's aluminum bed is wheeled out of an elevator, past two gurneys full of plasma and glucose, around one corner, then another, and down the short hallway toward the delivery room. One nurse keeps the IV bottle steady; a second holds a small damp towel against Shelley's forehead.

"She's contracting at about ninety now," says one of the nurses.

Shelley breathes quickly—once a second—and hard through her mouth. She is sweating.

"Because these spontaneous—"

Shelley grits her teeth and says "Shit."

They enter the delivery room. Two masked orderlies hoist Shelley up off the bed—one holds her calves, the other reaches under her armpits—and ease her onto the delivery table.

"She's started now, breaking through."

Dr. Traisman holds a stethoscope against the lower part of her abdomen. He listens, then moves it to another position.

"Try to relax now, honey," says one of the nurses. She holds Shelley's arm. "Just try to relax."

Another contraction arrives. Shelley winces.

"We've got four or five centimeters here of dilation," says Traisman.

The steady drip from the IV bottle continues.

"What about the new suture."

"Broke right through it again."

"A McDonald's?"

"Broke right through it."

Traisman places Shelley's left ankle into a stirrup and the second nurse raises the other one. Both legs glisten with sweat.

The contraction subsides but is followed right away by another one. Shelley cries out briefly and winces.

"Get me that—"

Shelley's whole abdomen quivers. She gasps.

"There."

Traisman gently parts Shelley's labia minora and touches the top of the skull.

"Oh, fuck . . . shit Jesus," says Shelley. She is sobbing now. "Oh, my God!"

Another spasm and thrust and the top two thirds of the head is exposed.

"Oh, my God!"

A nurse mops off Shelley's forehead.

"My   oh my   God . . ."

Traisman and the nurses work now in silence.

A third nurse enters the room and sees what is happening. She quickly goes out.

Traisman grabs the nine-inch-long female fetus and eases it the rest of the way out of Shelley's vagina.

Shelley tries catching her breath, but she can't. She calls out Jack's name.

Still holding on to the fetus, Traisman cuts the umbilical cord with a pair of surgical scissors and looks up at Shelley.

She sniffles and sobs. A nurse takes the fetus and leaves.
"It's all right now, Shelley. It's okay."

Another contraction, accompanied by a gurgling sound, and the afterbirth splashes out onto the floor.

"It's okay."

Exley's face, facing left, in the light from the thin slice of moon.
 Exley's eyes.

Andrewjewski talks on the phone. "He's talking . . . no, to . . . sure . . . sure. You can say that whatever . . ."
He listens for twenty-five seconds.
"Now listen," he says.

THE ALUMINUM hospital bed.

Beside it, on top of a small Formica table: two laundry receipts, a pitcher, a hairbrush, a water glass, a gray plastic tray with a spoon on it.

The steady drip of the IV bottle into the coil.

Corduroy slippers on the seat of the chair; a bathrobe draped over the back.

The closed closet door. The TV slung down from the ceiling. The coatrack.

Dozens of cards, seven plants, and various arrangements of flowers crowding the eight-foot-long windowsill.

On its side, on the table on the other side of the bed: Shelley's purse.

And Shelley, not moving, a blanket and sheet tucked neatly over her shoulders, her head on a pillow, hair matted back off her forehead, glazed eyes staring straight up.

A CROWDED CHEVROLET station wagon moves north on Sheridan Road. To the right the sky over Lake Michigan has begun to light up; to the left it is still mostly dark. It is quiet.

The WAIT news is on the car's radio with the volume turned low. A middle-aged woman is driving, her teen-aged son is sitting up front with her, and four or five younger girls are crowded into the back. They are quiet.

Three small birds call to each other as the cold slow dawn light spreads itself over the sky.

The boy holds up a green three-by-five card, looks out the window, and points. "This is it."

The wagon slows down, almost stops, then turns into the driveway marked "1900."

Two special agents dash across the white glaze of dew on the lawn and meet the car halfway up the driveway, signaling for the driver to stop. Frances starts barking.

The woman stops her car, rolls down her window, starts speaking to one of the agents.

Andrewjewski and Exley come out the front door.

The wagon now slowly proceeds up the driveway with the two agents trotting beside it.

Exley tries to see into the car as it comes toward the

porch, but all he can make out are the silvery reflections of tree limbs and sky flickering back over the windshield. He tries hard to focus.

The woman bears right as the driveway circles in front of the house. She stops by the porch, just in front of where Exley is standing. The agents stand back on the lawn.

Exley now faces the wagon's side windows, and the glare disappears. Andrewjewski goes around to the driver's side.

The five young girls in the back crowd as close as they can to the windows, yawning, talking, staring up at the house. Three have blond hair. Four of the five have on tennis clothes under their bulky down vests. Two are eating granola bars.

"We were just on our way to their six-thirty lesson," says the woman, passing the three-by-five card out the window to Andrewjewski. "It had this address . . ."

The smallest girl in the car now pushes her way past the others and looks out the window at Exley.

He realizes that

"She's just standing there, all by herself, you know, on our corner, though I never assumed . . ."

it's Elizabeth.

Shelley attempts to sit up as Elizabeth approaches her bed. Exley and two of the nurses are doing their best to get her to stay where she is, to watch her IV, to relax. She finally makes it up on one elbow, pushes her blanket and sheet back, then turns herself sideways and winces as Elizabeth climbs in beside her. They hug.

Exley sits on the edge of the bed. He kisses Elizabeth, pushes a damp strand of hair off her temple. The nurses go out. He holds Shelley's forearm and massages the small of her back.

Shelley clears her throat, tries to say something, can't. She tries again, can't. She brushes Elizabeth's hair off her forehead.

Exley gets up now and goes to the door. He pushes it all the way closed. He just stands there.

Elizabeth whispers three or four words to her mother, gulps, and starts sobbing.

"I know," Shelley says. She holds her more tightly. "I know."

Elizabeth tries to keep talking.

"I know."